In The Camp

Jean Bayle

Contents

Chapter One

I glanced nervously at my father stood next to me. After the horrific train journey, where we had been crushed impossibly close, the smell of over-heating human flesh unbearable; not to mention the human faeces from where people hadn't been able to wait until the end of the trip, which had taken many hours, we stood on the ramp.

Coming from the small town of Ajka, in the Hungarian mountains, to the Auschwitz camp, the letters scratched into the side of the train carriages informed us, in what I assumed to be Germany, going by the accents, had been oppressive and it had felt great to stretch my legs when we reached the other end; despite knowing this wasn't somewhere I wanted to be under any circumstances.

I didn't have any choice though. The SS Officers had raided the village, training a gun on anybody who had so much as stepped a foot out of place. Terrified and barely in control of my actions, I'd clambered into the train like a zombie, gripping my dad in an attempt to keep my sanity.

We were now stood in an impossibly large line, where Jewish men, women and children, like myself, were being crammed. It wound from the train we had got out of nearly an hour ago, for about half a mile in the other direction, where I could just about make out two men sitting at a desk.

Many officers were surrounding us, all laden with guns for if there were any trouble causers. I could see people who were nearly falling over, either from exhaustion or dehydration I wasn't sure, but it wasn't a pleasant sight. My heart went out to all of them. They must have been some of the people already boarded on the train when it came to Ajka, having suffered even longer.

Our village wasn't particularly large and the population consisted of people who couldn't afford the desirable houses located in some of the bigger cities. We weren't quite a mud-hut tribe, but the houses weren't big and were equally poor in the way they were furnished. Being high up in the mountains, we normally avoided any kind of contact from the outside world, but apparently today was an exception.

There was barely any speaking and a deathly silence was settled over the crowd of people; only broken by the occasional scream as someone fell to the floor - unconscious or dead I didn't want to know.

As we got closer to the two men, I noticed a trend in what happened. After them, were a further two lines and it was easy to work out who ended up where.

In the first line were a selection of boys and girls who looked about my age, seventeen, to about twenty-five. In the second line, was an array of children, the elderly, pregnant women and an assortment of other people who hadn't been put into the first line. I was confused as to why there were two lines and from the looks on everyone's faces, neither were positive.

I gripped my father's arm tighter, already knowing there was a big chance I could be separated from him. At the age of fifty-four, he most definitely did not fit into the first category, whereas I did. Having said that, many the same age as me could be identified in the second line as well. If I was lucky, I might also be selected for that line. I just wanted to stay with my father, he was the only person I had left now.

I had never really had any other family. My mother died during childbirth and so I was raised solely by my dad. She had never had any other children before me and my dad never remarried. He was crazily in love with my mother, I could tell that just by the way he talked about her, his voice filled with so much awe as he reminisced. I always wished I had known her, even if just for a while, because she must have been an amazing person for my dad to love her so much.

I'd had friends in the village, but as we piled onto the train, we'd been separated and I'd lost them now. Judging by the size of the ominous building in front of me, I knew it would probably be forever.

After another half an hour of silence, I was finally presented before the two men behind the desk. Unlike I expected, there was no paperwork or anything like that. Instead, the table was filled with an ashtray, because nearly everybody smoked, and some glasses of whisky. Although I didn't drink alcohol, even I could appreciate what it would feel like to have any form of liquid quenching my undeniable thirst.

The men themselves were dressed in smart army uniforms, complete with hats and badges adorning their jackets. The first looked smug and arrogant as he eyed me up. He leaned forward and across the desk slightly to leer at me closer, causing me to inch backwards automatically. I knew I wasn't ugly and had had several local boys courting me back in the village. I had never been interested though. I didn't want to be married, I was only 17. I still had a life to live, or at least I'd thought I had. Maybe I should have married, at least then I could have been with child and be guaranteed a spot in the same line my father would be joining.

"She's a pretty one." The first officer rasped with a heavy German accent. His voice was slimy and made me want to back away further. I held my stance though, because I didn't want to seem weak in front of these men. One of my main problems was my stubbornness and I got the impression it wasn't going to do me any good in this place; judging by the way they had treated us so far.

I took in the second soldier when he replied with a slight grunt. His hat was slightly askew and revealed some brown hair, cut in a style I wasn't accustomed to. Most men in the village grew their hair long, then tied it at the back to keep it out of the way. This man's, however, was short and whisked across the side of his face to cover up his forehead. It came just below his ears and I had to admit that it suited his young face. He must have only been about twenty and appeared very awkward when the first officer, who was considerably older, probably mid-thirties, addressed him.

The second officer's eyes raked over me then, causing a different feeling to ignite inside me. It was still understandably uneasy, I'd never had a man look at me that way before in this kind of situation, it brought about a sense of intrigue as well though. The way this man was looking at me was not the same as the first official, it didn't hold the same sleazy quality - the look that made you think he was going to harm me if he could get his hands on me.

My dad still stood next to me and as I moved closer to him for the support I knew his presence would bring, they seemed to finally notice him. "In that line." The seedy soldier ordered him, pointing to the line I'd already known my father would be joining. They still hadn't told me to move anywhere though, so I didn't. I didn't want to be any worse off than I already was.

I felt empty without my dad beside me though and the confident exterior I was presenting began to crumble under their examining gazes. They broke out in German conversation that I couldn't even begin to translate. I knew Hungarian, it being my first language, but German was lost on me. I got the feeling our only coinciding language was English.

When they broke off, both looking at me with blank faces, the second officer with the kinder eyes pointed to the opposite line to my dad's. I almost, almost, protested, not believing I was being separated from my only family. I caught the warning glares though and kept my mouth shut, trudging towards the shorter line. This was not before I gave one last fleeting look at my father. He gave me an encouraging smile, but I did not miss the tear the slid down his face, or the reciprocating one that glided down my own.

I joined the back of the queue that led into one half of the industrial looking building. I figured that it wasn't only a one building compound, but at the moment, it spread so wide it was the only thing I could see, other than the barbed wire fences and brick walls which blocked any kind of escape people would have been stupid enough to attempt.

It was all so grey and man-made looking that it brought about a sense of foreboding. I didn't want to enter under any circumstances, but that wasn't my decision to make. I also didn't want my head blasted off by the intimidating guns the soldiers carried with them.

I glanced at the other people surrounding me. They all looked terrified and were either glancing back at their loved ones in the other line, tears running down their faces, obvious distress marked on their faces, or were staring straight ahead, refusing to give people the satisfaction of seeing them so alone and scared.

I could see maybe one or two people who were actually talking to friends or relatives who they appeared to already know. That proved how many less people were in this line than the other. I recognised nearly everyone in the line with my father when I looked back out of curiosity. When I let my eyes browse down this queue, however, I picked out only one person who looked vaguely familiar.

I couldn't work out whether that was a good or bad thing. All I knew is that I wanted desperately to be in the other line, with my dad.

This queue was moving fast and I soon found myself being hurried along by the person behind me, as I was too busy taking in my surroundings and being unresponsive with shock. When we reached the front, another couple of soldiers were present, holding out ragged clothes for us to put on. What I did not realise was where we were expected to change. I watched in horror as the individuals in front of me stripped off and replaced their old clothes with the new ones provided.

When it got to my turn, I was nearly frozen solid. I knew everyone else had done it, felt the same humiliation as I had, but it was still terrifying. As I grabbed the flimsy dress that reminded me of a curtain or potato sack, I tried to convince myself that I had to do this. It was this or death I decided, as I once again noticed the guns, within a moment's movement, located on the officer's belts. As everyone else did the same, I tried to be as quick as possible. From watching the previous group, I realised there was going to be no underwear and this just made it even more unbearable.

For the couple of seconds I was fully naked, it felt as if everyone's eyes were on just me. I knew no one was probably even paying me any attention, but if felt as if everyone was examining me intently. It just made me pull on the material even faster. It came down to my knee and just above my breasts. Without any form of underwear, they were drooping and felt very uncomfortable, as well as making me incredibly self conscious. I knew I didn't have the smallest breasts and once again I felt as if everyone was solely taking in my appearance.

I hurried forward, my feet now bare against the uneven Earth and followed the gaggle of people I was grouping myself with. The next stop I could see we were approaching, was people being tattooed on the arm.

I had never even considered having a tattoo, it was considered unfeminine and I doubted I would have had any intention of having one even if I was a man. I knew this wasn't optional though and when I saw it was a sequence of numbers being shot into the skin with indelible ink, I realised it was a form of identification. I had wondered why there was no paperwork in the first place, but I understood now. There was no need for names when a much simpler form of cataloguing could be achieved.

I wondered if it hurt. There were no sounds of pain coming from the victims of the tattooists, but from the expressions on their faces, I could guess it wasn't pleasant - they were probably just too scared to actually express their pain vocally.

I took my seat nervously in front of a man dressed in the standard uniform for all the officers I had seen so far. The only difference this time was that he was equipped with a sharp needle used for permanently marking me. I somehow doubted her was a professional and could predict that he wasn't particularly concerned whether he hurt me or not.

I tried not to squirm in anticipation and when I finally did feel the cool metal against my skin, I had to smother my cry of surprise. It felt as if I had been zapped with a boiling piece of metal. I was surprised they hadn't cauterised me instead. It got slightly more tolerable as he moved around, but I didn't know how I was going to endure seven numbers. It was still stinging uncontrollably.

When he had finished, my arm was numb. I had barely felt the last couple of digits due to my arm being unintentionally anaesthetised. I took a look at the seven integers now embedded in my skin. 0134565. Did that mean I was nearly the one hundred and thirty-five thousandth inmate here? I looked around the cold building again and wondered how far it actually stretched. From the looks of it, it could easily hold that many people. Why someone would want to though, was not so simple to answer.

At the next stage, I was hurried through, not actually having to do anything, but watch what some other people were having to deal with. The boys were having their head's shaved, but I was grateful I got to keep mine. I had always loved my naturally wavy dark brown hair, which flowed down to the middle of my back. Even if the reason was because "the officers found women with long hair a commodity" I was happy I didn't need to be shaved. Some of the girls with short hair had had theirs removed.

The next step in this awful journey was being shown our accommodation. This was when we finally reached the end of the building and opened back into the fresh air. Laid out in front of us, were a selection of small huts, each with people identical to our group, only thinner and sicker looking, resting outside of them. The huts themselves also looked sick and thin and were crumbling, so that it appeared a small gust of wind would demolish them completely.

I could identify what was an almost sympathetic look in the other inmate's eyes as they watched us pass silently. I took in their skeletal forms and prayed to God that I wouldn't suffer the same fate. I wanted more than ever to be back in that other line now; to have been rejected by the two officers as a suitable candidate for this gaggle of people and to be safe in the arms of my father.

Our group of about sixteen women were shown our own hut then - we had been separated from the men, who would have their own lodgings presumably on the other side of this. It looked to be about the size of my bedroom back home, which wasn't particularly large, and was packed full with many bunk beds, top to toe, down each wall. There was barely enough room to manoeuvre around the room, but at least if I did end up that undernourished, being able to move around my new shelter would become less of a hassle.

When the SS officers departed and we were left to our own devices, under the strict instruction to not venture too far from our house because as soon as tonight was over, we'd be being put straight to work, I went to stand outside our hut.

The baking sun beat down on me, making my pale skin heat up and transforming it into an unnatural shade of pink. I had always burnt easily, so being exposed to the German summer sun wasn't going to treat my body well. I was happy to soak it up whilst it lasted though, I got the feeling I wouldn't be seeing it often.

As I watched the clouds float across the sky, wondering how on Earth I had gotten into this situation, I found myself blinking back the tears I managed to hold in thus far. I missed my dad already and wondered desperately if I would ever see him again. He'd been the only constant in my life and to think of him being gone had reduced me to a blubbering wreck.

Then, I heard someone call my name and I was forced to regain my composure.

"Viktória?"

Chapter Two

C hapter Two...

A shrill voice carried to my ears and my head snapped up. I would recognise that tongue anywhere and it shot a thrill through me to know that I wasn't completely alone. "Stephánia?" I cried, staring in awe as she ran over and hugged me senseless. "I can't believe you're here too!"

Knowing that I wasn't completely isolated in this hell hole and at least had one friend to communicate with had made my terrible day just a tiny bit more bearable. I still missed my dad, but maybe I would be able to see him again sometime soon. He'd been put into a separate line, but he had to be being kept somewhere in this giant structure. Keeping that thought in mind gave me some sort of inspiration to keep my composed exterior, at least for a little while longer.

"I thought I'd lost you when the officers raided the village, I'm so glad I get to see you again!" She exclaimed, finally releasing me from the bone crushing hug she'd enveloped me in. "What number are you?" She inquired, bringing back the realisation that my arm still stung painfully from where the needle had marked it.

I didn't have a sleeve anymore, in the flimsy potato sack dress we'd been given, so it didn't take a lot of effort for me to twist and show Stephánia the seven small numbers embellished in a band around the top of my arm.

She didn't look at all concerned about having a row of digits as our form of identification rather than our birth names, whereas I was furious about it. Whatever made them think they could change how we were known and wipe us clean of our identities was clearly misinformed. This had been the name both my mother and father had decided on before I was born - it was the only thing I owned that related to my mother, no German official, no matter how great they thought they were, was going to get away with that.

"We're only a few numbers apart." Stephánia interrupted my mental tirade. That made me realise that barely anyone in our village must have been put into this line. There had already been people in the train when we'd been herded on, but if me and Stephánia were this close in our numbers, then only a select few must have been chosen to enter this side of the camp. I would have felt honoured, if it wasn't for the knowledge that I could have been with my father on the other side.

"That is weird." I commented. "So do you know what this place actually is yet?" I inquired, deciding it was time to do some investigating. We might be under close supervision and I already knew that I didn't want to get on the wrong side of the guards, but that didn't quench the thirst I had, both literal and mental, to discover what it was exactly that I was doing here. This clearly wasn't a desirable place to end up and we hadn't come by choice, so why were we here?

I was obviously aware of the war raging on around us. It had been going on for three years now, since 1939, but being the small village that we were, we'd avoided being in any direct conflict.

Hungary was part of the Axis Powers and we were allied with Germany, Austria and Italy - another factor that added to my confusion. By the looks of it, we were some kind of war prisoner, but Germany were supposed to be on our side. I could easily recognise that the inmates were Jewish, bar maybe a handful in my vision, and that proved to be some kind of explanation.

Hungary's government consisted of many anti-Semitic individuals, one of the main reasons we resided in such an out of the way town. Being against the Jewish population had caused higher ranking leaders to label us as outcasts and our lifestyle had been affected by it.

"I've got no idea, but I've met some pretty nice people so far. My room-mates are really friendly, you should come and talk to them with me." She suggested.

I sighed. Stephánia had always been far too optimistic for my liking. Whereas I found the negatives in nearly all situations and had to put a pessimistic view onto everything, Stephánia could be positive, find the best possible outcome, then convince herself that was how it would turn out. Sometimes I wished I could be like that, and sometimes I knew I would just be setting myself up for eternal misery if I ever became that idealistic.

"Okay, sure." I decided that bringing her down wasn't the way to go about this and I should be happy that she kept the buoyant attitude she had adopted, despite my growing doubts as to how we would be finding our stay.

Of course I had been expecting us to be being hauled away to somewhere bad in the first place, but never to this extent. When we'd been gathered onto the already overcrowded train, I hadn't been anticipating there to be a positive outcome at the end of it. Then we had reached the camp and my initial thoughts had been reinforced and simply by the foreboding atmosphere the building had given off, I knew this place was bad news. I was starting to realise that it was even worse than that now though.

The images of the skeletal people we had passed on the way here were burned into my mind, constantly reminding me that I was going to end up like that. They were dreadfully undernourished and clearly not far off death. Having said that, if I ended up like that, death might become an appealing alternative.

Their clothes had been even more bedraggled than the feeble garments we were currently donning; it was clear we wouldn't get a replacement so I needed to keep this one in the best condition I could.

Another noticeable feature that I took in was their bare feet. I had assumed we'd be provided with new shoes, or at least replacement shoes, but that had never happened and I now gathered that it wasn't going to. My feet hurt already from walking on the dry, uneven Earth that the camp seemed to be built upon and if this work we were expected to do involved lots of walking then I would most definitely be in a lot of agony.

I followed Stephánia towards her own hut which was two down from my own. Surveying the place I guessed I would be calling home for the foreseeable future, I wondered if the bigger picture looked the same as my eye could see.

Despite the variety of colours, everything seemed grey to me. The endless rows of insanely small huts for the number of people who were supposed to be residing in them stretched out as far as I could determine. I had been used to small sleeping arrangements, but this was going a bit too far. Even I couldn't understand the need to have sixteen people in such a small room when there was an extensive area of land surrounding me.

When we reached the hut Stephánia was staying in, several other girls were sitting around, all looking extremely morbid and depressed. They looked up when we entered and the one closest to the door mumbled a greeting in Hungarian. There were several different nationalities here, so it was easier to just stick to English. I had been fluent in it all my life and so it posed no problem to me.

I sat down on one of the lower levels of a bunk bed near the door. They had all come in on the same train as me and Stephánia, so they were just as uninformed as I was. I was grateful for the rest, but I couldn't help but think that there wasn't going to be much opportunity for me to do it after tonight.

"Whereabouts are you all from?" I asked, deciding to break the silence that was setting the mood of misery.

There were a chorus of deviating countries, varying from Germany, to the Netherlands, to Hungary - like myself. It made me wonder how long some people had actually spent on that train and consider myself lucky that I'd been on the last stop before being forced into this bleak camp.

After deciding that there was no one here who was actually willing to talk about anything in more than antisocial grunts, I turned to Stephánia and queried her on what happened to her family.

Unlike me, she had an extended family, consisting of both mother, father, older brother and two younger twin sisters. They had always been close and I knew she'd probably be taking this just as badly as me, despite her relatively cheery appearance.

"Do you know what happened to your family, when you went up to the desk with the two officers behind it?"

She shook her head. "My brother got put into the same line as me, but they separated us from the boys so I don't know where he is now. My parents got put into the other line, but something weird happened to my sisters." She explained. I gave her a puzzled look. I understood everything else that she'd said, but what happened to her sisters? Being so much younger, at the age of twelve, I assumed that they'd just be put into the same line as her parents. "One of the men went wild when he saw them. They called some new soldiers and they took them away."

My frown deepened. What were the soldier's intentions with the twins? I had always found it fascinating that Stephánia's sisters were identical, who wouldn't?, but I didn't think it would make them a special case when it came to line selection on the ramp.

I didn't want to upset Stephánia any more than I guessed she was already though and didn't push it. "Did your dad end up in the same line as my parents?" She checked, already knowing the answer.

The constricting pain in my chest intensified at the thought of my father and what he would be doing now. Would he be in the same cramped conditions? Would he be missing me too? Would he have found someone that he knew from the village like I had? Maybe he'd have found Stephánia's parents and they'd be having a similar conversation to the one we were having now.

"Yeah." I answered simply, not feeling the need to elaborate and bring up such a painful topic. I knew Stephánia would be feeling the same pang, but she was more open than me and was more willing to discuss her feelings, whereas I would bottle them up inside me and hope they would just go away.

Stephánia shot me a sympathetic look, obviously understanding the inner turmoil commencing within my mind. I wanted to rebel. I wanted to scream and cry at the loss of my father. I hadn't been without him for more than a day nearly all my life and the idea that I might not see him anytime soon cut deeper than the tattoo had and was far more distressing.

I wanted to escape this awful place. Even though I knew I hadn't even seen the half of it yet, felt even a fraction of the terror I knew I was going to have to endure, it was already the worst experience I'd ever been through.

It was worse than when my best friend of ten years had died of typhoid when I was fifteen. Adrian had been the one person I had shared everything with and when he had been diagnosed with the dreadful disease, I had been devastated. That was nothing compared to the agonising grief I had endured after his death though.

It had been arranged for us to marry when I came of age at sixteen and he was the one person I was willing to commit to. I had rejected any other offers after his death on the basis that I owed it to him.

I hadn't loved him in the respect that I often read about. Famous novelists always created the image of love with such an intensity I always thought impossible, but if it was true, then I never had it with Adrian. We had shared many kisses secretly, but the fireworks I so often dreamed about had never been present.

I had enjoyed them though and I had enjoyed being with Adrian, he had listened to me and understood all of my problems, the interpretation had been reciprocated. When he died, I promised myself I wouldn't give myself away to anyone I felt less towards than I did Adrian. He was the person I was basing all my ideal man's attributes on. I wouldn't let anyone replace him. No one could fill the hole Adrian had left following his death.

Weighed down by my depressing thoughts and unbearable memories, I decided it was time for me to get some rest. It was still only early on in the day, but I had been up early aiding my father with some of the housework. His back was becoming a problem for him and so he was relying on me more and more. I didn't mind though, I wanted him to stay in good health for as long as possible.

A sudden thought came to me. If we were being put to work in the morning, would the people in the other line also being forced into labour? Maybe that was the reason they'd separated us. Because we were the ones physically able, whilst the others would be used for more mental tasks, like calculations or writing.

I sighed heavily and stood up, stretching my arms above my head before realising that my extremely short dress-like garment was riding up to an even more inappropriate place. I flushed slightly and instantly lowered my arms, despite knowing no one was probably paying me any attention.

"I'm going to settle down in my own bed." I informed Stephánia who nodded, laying down on her own bed in turn. She had had an equally tough journey today, if not worse having been separated from all of her family members. rather than the one I was missing and I could comprehend how she was feeling.

I traipsed back to my own shelter, feeling the setting sun on my tired face as it heated my already boiling body even further. I was thoroughly missing my home town and was hoping to wake up any time soon, to realise this was all just a dream and reality was a different case altogether.

All I knew was that if this was a dream, I would definitely appreciate what I had in Ajka more when I woke up.

Here is the next chapter. I'm not sure how much you know about the Holocaust, but I find it really interesting and I'm trying to keep it as historically correct as I can do, minus some obvious points. I find it really fascinating though and love writing about it, even if people aren't interested in reading about it :)

Thanks for the votes and comments, much appreciated! :D

Chapter Three

C hapter Three...

A lot of shouting and an extremely high pitched whistle was what woke me up the next morning, early morning at that. The sun had barely risen in the sky and without the aid of lights, it proved a difficult task being able to see.

I had slept in the dress, not wanting to be fully naked beneath the flimsy sheet we had been provided with. Despite the weather being warm during the daylight hours, it was considerably cooler at night and even though I'd kept my garment on, I had been shivering and goose bumps had still littered my skin.

Regardless of my internal complaints and desperate need to close my eyes and drift off into another deep sleep, I hurried along in the same fashion as everyone else, determined not to stand out among the crowd. Another factor affecting my sudden movement was the SS-officers who stood at the door, both armed - one with a gun and the other with the incessant whistle.

After glancing around quickly for my shoes, I realised that I didn't have any. That dimmed my non-existent enthusiasm even more and the scowl on my face deepened yet further.

I still scurried out the door with the other girls who shared my dorm though and soon found myself in a disorderly line consisting of many other hut's inmates as well. I spotted Stephánia further behind me, but was far too intimidated by the officials who were currently observing the line and trying to make it more organized to move back to her and settled for a wave instead. With the threat of being shot hanging over everyone's heads, that wasn't too much of a trial.

Apparently Stephánia wasn't bothered though and began pushing her way though the thinning crowds, making her way towards me. She was stopped in her tracks though when a general stepped purposely in front of her.

From my position I could see every gory detail of what happened as he demanded where she thought she was going. I was stock still when she pointed to me and smiled sweetly at the man, obviously not realising how dangerous of a situation she was in. Disobeying any orders from these men was a decidedly bad idea and Stephánia was a fool for thinking that it wasn't.

The stout man who had prevented her from walking any further twisted around until his ghastly face caught mine. He gave me a sleazy smile before turning back to Stephánia. In one quick motion, he had slapped her across the face. "You do not do anything, without being told to first." He informed her sharply, before returning to his place observing the line.

Stephánia, who had been knocked sideways by the sheer force of the blow, staggered and then stood upright again. She didn't dare to look up and meet my eyes, but I didn't miss the drop of water that dripped from her face and onto the ground.

I had realised that this place was bad, but not so dreadful that I risked being subject to violence because I stepped out of line - literally. That thought scared me even more. If such a simple act resulted in such harsh treatment, then what would happen if someone did something seriously wrong? I'd thought the guns were simply a sign of authority, meant to scare us, but I now realised they were for much more than that and I wouldn't be surprised if I witnessed them being used.

I shuffled forward in the now organised row of people and wondered where we were headed. Maybe we would be working on the half of the camp where my father was. Even a glimpse of him would be enough for me, just to know he was okay. I knew I wouldn't be that lucky though and so I didn't get my hopes up.

We were halted after about five minutes rapid walking and an officer at the front began ordering us about and splitting us up into groups. Much like when we'd first arrived, we reached a desk and were told to go either one way or the other.

I noticed a trend in who was going where once again and noted that Stephánia was likely to be in my group. It was mainly men, or the strong women, that were placed in the second line. People who had physical strength were being chosen, whilst the rest of us were deposited into the first line. Whilst I was perfectly healthy, my slender frame wasn't packing much muscle and was therefore not picked to be in the second line. I wasn't disappointed though, because I wasn't looking forward to the idea of manual labour.

When we reached our destination, a short but wide grey looking building, we were told to gather around the main officer who was dishing out instructions. He was holding a pair of spectacles in his hand. "You will be separating the glass from the metal." He informed us. "It may hurt your hands, but you will not complain." He finished, before leading us into another room.

I was instantly taken aback by the sight in front of me. An enormous pile of various types of glasses was against the wall, with things resembling troughs around the outside in pairs. I recognised them as where to we were to put the rims and lenses. There were no seats however and I doubted we'd be allowed to sit down. I wondered how long we would be working for, because I didn't know how long I could stand up for.

My thoughts instantly went to my father. He had worn an old pair of glasses and was lost without them - blind as a bat. If they had taken his off him, how would he be coping. I guess there was no point in taking them off someone if they couldn't see without them though, because what use was an almost blind person to these men? I also realised that no one who had been in our group had worn spectacles.

After giving each of us a station, he left the room. That didn't mean we were alone though, a number of other officers were still spread around the room, stood against various places along the wall.

There was a mixture of appearances as my eyes scanned across them all. From short and reasonably plump looking men, to the tall and strong ones. Even when all clad in the same uniform, it was still easy to pick out who held which characteristics.

I had only seen a handful of soldiers close enough to gauge their facial features, but I instantly recognised one of the ones present today. It was the same soldier that had been at the desk when we first arrived.

He was stood against the wall, back straight and arms folded behind him. I could clearly see the gun holstered against his side and the way his hat was slightly askew on his head, revealing a smidgen of his brown hair that I found oddly attractive.

Despite his stiff posture, I could clearly see his eyes surveying the room. They didn't just flick past when they reached me though and our gazes locked in an intense stare. He didn't just scan my body and give it an appreciative look though, his gaze didn't even waver from my face.

Just like last time, it provoked the sense of intrigue and I wondered why he was looking at me in such a way none of the other soldiers seemed capable of. His sparkling grey eyes pierced into mine, but held no cruelty like the others'. He didn't give me a look that was sleazy or sordid in anyway, much the opposite actually. His look was almost sympathetic.

I snapped my eyes away though when I realised I should be working. Any slacking off would no doubt be rewarded with some form of punishment and I wasn't as willing to get backhanded as Stephánia had appeared to be.

So, I set to work with the tedious assignment ahead of me. I picked up a pair of glasses and considered how I should approach the task in hand. Weighing it over in my mind, I decided to go about it in the way I decided was most conventional. I attempted to push the glass out of the rims.

To my utter surprise, it simply popped out and fell onto the floor with an almost incoherent thud. I picked it up and shrugged, before dropping it into the correct trough, then tried the same technique with the other lens. It was just as successful and despite the sullen situation, I found a smile creeping its way onto my face. As least if I complete the task without too much hassle it would be a lot less of a burden.

After what must have been a couple of hours, my legs were beginning to ache. I had also realised my method wasn't quite as foolproof as I'd first deduced. I was now sporting several small lacerations to both hands and even one on my arm. I had managed to get that when one of the lenses I'd been attempting to remove had shattered and propelled everywhere, including my arm.

It wouldn't have been particularly painful if I'd been able to stop working and simply rest my bloody hands, but obviously that wasn't an option. Instead I'd carried on, resulting in aggravating the gashes and making them wider, as well as creating new ones.

I didn't know how long we'd be working for, but I hoped we would be finished soon. My first issue was the dull pain in my hands, of course. The second was the complaints my legs were making at supporting my weight for such a lengthy time. I wouldn't be so aggravated if we could have done this sitting down, even on the floor.

That wouldn't have solved my third problem of having an increasingly full bladder, however. Only one person had asked to use a lavatory and that had been about half an hour ago. They'd been timid and shy whilst inquiring and definitely regretted it when they spoke. After receiving some verbal abuse and a pair of glasses thrown in their face, it had been clear no one would be attending the toilet.

The men who had been placed in this area to work had simply urinated on the floor, receiving no complaints from the officers. For girls, which were the majority of us, it had proved to be a lot more complicated. I had witnessed a couple squatting on the floor and satiating their needs however, much to my disgust.

Another hour passed and I was thankful when the general who had distributed our commands returned to the room. My stomach was rumbling uncomfortably loudly and I felt as though everyone had been able to hear it. I was only expecting to be given meagre rations though, if any, going by the malnutrition the emaciated figures, that hadn't quite been banished from my subconscious, had clearly undergone.

When I got to the long awaited toilet, I found myself in yet another line. It seems as though everyone had needed to use the lavatory and I would be lucky if I even got a go before we were being forced to decapitate some more spectacles.

When I finally reached the loo, I almost retched in disgust. Unlike at home, this was most definitely a public toilet. Waste was coated around the seat and there was no paper in sight. I observed it in horror and was very tempted to give in and simply urinate where I was working - it looked more sanitary.

Deciding I wasn't going to humiliate myself so publicly, I squatted nearly and inch above the seat and released my excess fluids. I had been dying to sit on the seat, simply for my legs to get a rest, but I'd rather collapse from the aches than sit on that nauseating, repulsive excuse for a seat.

Feeling very awkward and horrified at the idea people would think I'd contributed to the abomination in the toilet, I exited the little cabin it was situated in. There was still a substantial amount of people in the queue and I pitied the people who weren't going to have time to use it.

When I caught sight of the other main attraction people had swarmed to, I was deliriously happy. My parched throat became even drier at the sight of water that was being distributed throughout the workers. I scampered over to where it was being rationed out.

It was the same soldier who had caught my gaze earlier who was dishing out the precious liquid and I patiently joined the considerably shorter queue. I could guess that everyone had had water and then rushed off to the toilet, whereas I would rather be dehydrated than mortify myself by going to the bathroom on the floor in clear view of everyone else - especially the young officer.

When I did reach the front of the line, the young officer's eyes assessed me before pouring me some water. "There you go." He told me, his heavy German accent wrapping around me as he spoke with a surprising gentleness. I noticed he had also caught sight of my ensanguined hands and gave me a concerned look. It made something warm grow inside me, just at the knowledge he didn't examine me with disgust as many others would have done.

"Thank you." I replied, giving him one last glance, before turning around and letting the next person receive their measure. When they turned around, I noticed that they had a considerably smaller amount compared to my own and I quickly gulped some, allowing the cool liquid to run down my throat and make me sigh in contentment. I had really needed that drink and despite my still growling abdominal region, was feeling marginally better.

Once I had indulged myself in the last of the cherished liquid, I returned the container which had been holding it to the now unoccupied soldier. I handed it to him, rather shyly and was baffled when he gave me a breathtaking smile. "Danke Schön." He spoke in his native tongue, saying the words I vaguely recognised as thank you.

I gave him a hesitant smile back and scurried back to my work station. We had only been given about five minutes rest before being ushered back to our designated areas and being pushed to continue dismantling the pairs of glasses.

By the time it had gone dark, we had been given one more five minute rest, this time with the added bonus of a mouldy piece of bread to fill our famished stomachs. I was now dead on my feet and longed for the incommodious bed I was now residing in.

As we traipsed back to our less than efficient accommodation, I stumbled a couple of times. I would most definitely be enjoying the comfort of sleep tonight, hopefully with no interruptions. Working a ten-hour, non-stop, day had taken its toll on me and I didn't know if I'd be able to cope like this for a lengthy amount of time.

I collapsed onto my bunk as soon as I returned, listening to the other girls complain about their dreadful day. We had a rare case in our hut though. One of the girls had been selected as a physically able one and been chosen to go with the second line which hadn't helped us disassemble spectacles all day.

The other girls were therefore questioning her ruthlessly on what she had spent the day doing, assuming she had got it easier than the rest of us.

When she did reveal what she had been occupied with, it stunned us all into silence.

I actually loved writing that chapter! It was great to introduce the soldier a bit more, although I'm still stuck as to how they're going to get to know each other properly.

I'm sure some of you can guess what the physically able people will have been doing, but you can't have a story without some cliffhangers!

Like on my other story, I've got to mention this fan-fiction that I follow religiously. It's based on the game fable, but you don't need to have played it to appreciate the writing. It's beautifully written and by far one of the best things I've ever read. It's in the external link if anyone is interested :)

Oh, and this story was on the historical fiction what's hot list on page number 3! Wow! I was really happy to see that, so thanks to everyone who has voted! :D

Chapter Four

Chapter Four...

"When we got to our destination, an officer explained to us what we were expected to do." She shivered at the memory and I anticipated something dreadful that she was about to relive. "He told us, we'd be carrying...dead bodies."

I couldn't help the horrified gasp that escaped my mouth as I looked at her incredulously. I had expected maybe some cruel manual labour, such as moving bricks or hauling heavy objects - I had no idea that the hefty items would be human flesh.

She flinched in disgust as she recapped the day in her head, repulsive images no doubt clouding her mind. "We had to carry them to the crematorium where they were thrown into a furnace." She paused then and choked on a sob. "There were children." She informed us, shaking as one of the girls pulled her into a heartfelt hug.

I found myself speechless as she revealed that fact. Sure, I knew this place was despicable, but killing children was just taking it too far. To start off with, I was completely confused as to why there were so many dead bodies in the first place.

I had seen the undernourished inmates when we'd first arrived, but that wasn't enough to result in so many bodies, plus they weren't children. My thoughts instantly went over to the other camp. Were they being treated the same as us over there? Being fed minimal amounts and being kept in cramped conditions. I shuddered as I imagined my father in the same state.

He was generally a strong man, despite his age, and would okay for a couple of weeks, but I didn't want him to be suffering. If it came down to it, I would rather he was dead than enduring such a crippling illness, so to speak.

The girl was still crying helplessly into another one's shoulder when I decided it was time for me to go to sleep. I didn't need to stay up all night when I knew that there was going to be more gruelling work for me to be doing in the morning. I needed all the rest I could get in this place and that was a sure thing.

Yet, despite my knowledge and reasoning, I still found myself lying awake whilst everyone else enjoyed the comfort of sleep. I had observed as, gradually, everyone had made their way to their bunks and settled down. Everyone was now sleeping soundly and unaware of the world around them. I was still weighed down with the ominous feeling that something was terribly wrong, however.

So, I sat up, almost banging my head on the incredibly low ceiling and attempted to creep down the unstable ladder without disturbing the girl who was asleep below me. Apart from the slight creek as I finally reached the floor, after what seemed like the most treacherous journey I'd ever made, I tiptoed out to the doorway.

It hadn't been closed entirely and so I could peep out without touching it and risking anyone waking up and scolding me. When my legs began to ache, however, I braved it and inched the door open, ignoring the painful screech it made for a split second. I glanced anxiously around the room, checking for any disturbances and noticing none.

Slipping through the small crack I had made, I found myself embraced by the outside world. The weather wasn't perfect, but it was just about warm enough for me to be outside in my flimsy dress. It was dark and the moon was risen high in the sky, illuminating the surrounding area and allowing me to see the vast expanse of industrial looking buildings that spread either side of me.

If I strained my eyes, I could just make out a mountain rising above the complex in the distance. It was enough to reassure me that we weren't on another planet and that this wasn't a horrible version of Earth. It also served to remind me how insignificant I was in all of this and that we were very isolated here as well. If the nearest identifiable piece of the natural world was that far away from me, then I really was in a hellish version of reality.

Back in the village there'd been lots of nature surrounding us. Being so high up in the mountains we were surrounded by trees and smaller plants and often relied on them to uphold our lifestyle. Since we were so far away from any major civilisations, we were without some of the latest technology. For that reason, little things like rivers and plants were necessities when it came to surviving and having a good quality of life.

Being apart from any real wildlife was strangely frightening. There had been a tree on the outskirts of Ajka that I'd often gone to climb. I'd loved climbing trees and the thrill that came with the risk of being so high up. This tree had been an especially hard one to climb though with branches that extended so far out I didn't know which ones to trust and which ones would send me plummeting.

Always ready to accept a challenge, I had taken it on, determined to reach it at least close to the top. Apart from the odd scratch and gash, I'd finally done it. I'd hit home and grasped the top branch, letting the sense of achievement take over my body.

After Adrian's death, it had become a refuge for me and I used to climb it when I needed to be alone, knowing that no one else would have a hope in hell of reaching me at the top of it. I could do with a tree like that here. The only difference here would be that anyone underneath me would get a full view of my womanly parts.

I sighed, but it was soon mingled with a yawn as I covered my mouth out of habit. There wasn't anyone here to witness me being impolite, so it didn't really matter. My statement was proved to be incorrect however when I recognised a figure walking towards me.

I assumed it was just another prisoner like me, until I saw the hat adorning his head. Scrambling to my feet, I made an attempt to scurry back inside my hut and hope that the officer hadn't seen me. I didn't need the added issue of an SS officer deciding that he needed to punish through some inhumane method because I'd been outside my hut when I was supposed to be in bed.

I was never that fortunate however and his heavy German accent cut me off. "Wait?" He didn't so much as order, but ask. His voice wasn't commanding, but it sounded as though he was requesting that I didn't move.

I stood stock still, regardless of whether he was friendly or not. Either way I was too terrified that if I moved I would risk having a gun pulled on me. I didn't trust anyone around me, especially not a German officer.

He didn't pull any sort of fire arm from his person though and so I held my breath until he told me I could go. He just carried on approaching me though, not saying a word. As he got closer, I was shocked to admit that I recognised at him.

It was the same young official that had treated me to extra water earlier the same day. When he got within talking distance, close, but not too close, he offered me a small smile, that even in the doom and gloom seemed to cheer me up slightly. I hadn't seen so much as one happy face, aside from Stephánia, who was always far too optimistic, since I arrived. That wasn't counting the brilliant smile this same man had given me only this morning that had lightened the day considerably then and even though this was only a small smile, it was enough to get me to respond with a similar one.

It was only now that I realised how much taller than me he was. He towered above me, making my slender frame seem very insignificant. He must have been nearly six foot, but it didn't bother me. In fact, it seemed to add to his attractiveness - as did his muscles.

"Why are you out here so late?" He inquired, rather than accused like I had expected. He seemed genuinely curious and I could guess he didn't witness many inmates hanging around outside their accommodation when they could be enjoying some peaceful sleep.

I shrugged. "I couldn't sleep. This is rather a lot to take in." I explained, trying not to be too outspoken and end up in even more trouble than I was already in from just being here. This man might seem friendly enough, but I wasn't counting on anything. He could be setting me up for my downfall.

He sighed. "I know. I can't believe they're even doing this. It's horrific." He admitted, causing me to gape at him, shocked to the core.

"But..." I stammered out, unable to form a sentence. Someone who worked here, someone who was supposed to be upholding the law in this place, agreed that what was being undertaken here was despicable. Why would he even work here if he thought that? "But you work here!" I finally exclaimed, unable to contain my curiosity and surprise.

"Not out of choice." He revealed. I raised a questioning eyebrow at him. Before he answered though, he gestured to the step I had been previously sitting on, indirectly telling me to sit down. I did as he suggested, taking a seat and smoothing out the sack draped around me. He took a seat next to me. "My father worked against Hitler. He didn't believe in his regime and the way he was condemning people. He was part of Abwehr and one of the plans to assassinate Hitler. He was caught and taken prisoner and put through what I can only imagine was unbearable torture. As his son, I was automatically seen as a traitor. I was allowed to prove my loyalty by becoming a soldier, however. If I'd refused, I would have suffered the same fate as my dad." He explained, looking away from my eyes when he had finished and setting them downcast.

My instant reaction was to look down on him, to call him a coward for even being a part of this and not accepting the pain to show his loyalty to his father. "I know, I'm a coward. I couldn't do it though, I couldn't go through that torture." He muttered, as if he could read my mind. It sounded as though he was talking almost more to himself than me.

When it came down to the reality of the situation, however, and I tried to put myself in his shoes, I wondered how I'd deal with it. I loved my dad, more than anyone in the world, but would I be able to condemn myself to death, endure that unbearable affliction because of it. Or would I do the cowardly thing also. Refuse the pain, but be a part of something that I despised and betray the person who was my only family.

"I know why you did it." I said eventually, after weighing it up in my mind. "I'd do the same." I revealed.

His head snapped up and he looked at me curiously. "Why? What I did was unforgivable." He stated.

He obviously felt guilty for what he'd done, yet made no attempt to rectify it now. If he really wanted, then he could easily walk up to the soldiers, tell them that he couldn't do it any longer and even avoid the torture by using the gun in his belt to shoot himself. The fact that he hadn't assured me that he was just as afraid of death as he made out, no matter how bad the consequences of staying alive.

"Well, accepting your own death would be a hard thing, especially going through the agony that would no doubt come with it. I don't think I could make that decision knowing what would come with it." I explained.

I was still trying not to be too outspoken. This soldier might sound like he's telling me the truth, but anything he was spouting could be lies. I didn't trust a sole in this establishment, apart from Stephánia, and this officer was no exception.

He just shook his head. "You're too understanding." He informed me. "I almost wish you'd tell me how much of a gutless coward I am. That I should take this gun and put it to my head right now. I feel like I deserve it."

I looked across at him and our gazes locked together. I could see the remorse swimming in his eyes and in that moment, I did believe him. I believed everything he'd just said without questioning myself once. The amount of guilt in his face could not be faked and if it was, he should be an actor rather than a soldier.

I hesitated before asking the thing that had been bugging me since I'd even tried to go to sleep. "Can I ask you something?"

He looked up at me curiously, trying to gauge what type of question I was about to ask. He probably assumed it was about his father, but it was far from it. "Sure."

"This girl in our hut," I gestured to the building behind me, "she says that she spent the day, carrying…dead people." I felt an unstoppable shiver run up my spine at the thought of doing something so horrible.

I saw the officer's face paled and he averted his eyes once again. "She's telling the truth." He admitted. That wasn't really what I was trying to ascertain, however, I'd already gathered that she wasn't lying. What I was really interested in knowing is who they were and why there were so many of them.

He was obviously trying to avoid the subject and despite knowing I wasn't to overstep the mark, I couldn't help but push my luck. "Who are they?" I inquired cautiously, my words more drawn out than they would be normally, as I awaited a bad reaction.

"I don't think you'll want to know that." He told me sincerely.

I raised an eyebrow. "Why not? Isn't the fact that there dead bad enough?"

He shook his head, "It is dreadful and so much worse than that. I…I don't want to tell you." He finalised.

I glared at him. "Why not?" I demanded, completely forgetting my place for a moment and scowling. "I have a right to know don't I?"

It was his turn to scowl at me now. "Do you not think you should watch your tongue?" He snapped, startling me for a second. His voice was harsh and cold as he barked out the command. It made me realise that he'd been working here for probably a while and was more used to dealing with the inmates in a brutal manner than I'd anticipated. "Anyone but me would have abused you in some form for simply being outside this late."

I stayed silent, but could not force the grimace off my face. I knew I shouldn't have said that, in fact, I had been far too comfortable around this man. If I had been so stupid in front of any of the other officers, it would have resulted in a red mark being plastered against my cheek, and probably more. I needed to watch my mouth and remember I was not somewhere friendly.

He looked at me more tenderly. "I don't want you to get hurt and being too comfortable around the schutzstaffel is not something you should become." I recognised the full German word for SS, but it was hardly ever spoken when it could be shortened to two letters so easily. "If you do, it will end up being bad for you and I don't want you to get hurt."

The way in which that statement was said, with such sincerity it made my heart swell, was something I wasn't expecting to here out of a German's mouth any time soon. Or anyone's mouth to be fair. I had already established that I wouldn't be seeing my father any time soon and I was too terrified to speak with Stephánia again without risking her being harmed, or me for that matter.

"What's your name?" I asked suddenly, changing our conversation to something much more chatty and light. I was sick of the tension weighing down on me. Aside from that, I was also insanely curious to know what he was called.

"Jakob." He informed me, smiling slightly as he caught my eyes. "You?"

For some reason, I'd expected him to know my name, but I don't know why. The only real identification I had here was my number. I touched my arm absentmindedly where the tattoo was clearly visible against my milky white skin. "Viktória." I told him, my Hungarian accent becoming more pronounced as I spoke my name fluently.

"It's a nice name." He told me gently.

"Thanks."

Before we could make any further comments, another silhouette could just be seen in the distance. I already knew that it was an official and I stood up in an instant, Jakob following my lead. "I'd better go and you need to go inside." He told me, his voice rushed. "I hope to speak to you again, Viktória." The way my name rolled of his tongue in his heavy accent made my heart rate increase ever so slightly and I found myself wishing that he'd say it again.

Then he hurried away, no doubt to go and pursue the job he'd been supposed to be doing when he saw me.

I followed his command, entering the building and not caring if the squeaking door woke my roommates, I just needed to be away from who-ever it was that was coming.

Thankfully, I was safe and no one so much as stirred in their bunks. Hurriedly, I scrambled up to my bunk and fell asleep almost instantly.

Talking to Jakob had been an enlightening experience, in more ways than one.

Sorry for the wait, but I've had so many idea's for it's not a game of chance that I just had to write them down, I still loved writing the chapter though, and althout I was going to do this differently, I'm pleased with how it turned out. I don't want to rush things with this like I normally do, so I hope it's alright!

Thanks to the people who have read and enjoyed this story, although it's not got as many fans, I think the actual writing in it is a better quality than my other two stories!

Hope you enjoy :)

Chapter Five

C hapter Five...

I spent the next day thinking over what Jakob had explained to me last night, understanding his decision more and more each time I went over our conversation. Whilst this was much more fun that popping the glass out of spectacle's frames, it did result in me gaining many more scratches and gashes than yesterday.

Unfortunately, I didn't see Jakob whilst I was working and was given only a meagre portion of water compared to what I was granted with yesterday. It was wrong for me to even want to see him, but I couldn't help myself. In a way, I knew that was only fair and that I shouldn't be treated any better than everyone else, but it didn't stop me wishing I had more. A few mouthfuls was hardly enough to get me through the day; especially in the back breaking heat which seemed to have engulfed the camp.

I found my thoughts straying to the girl who had described her horrendous day carrying corpses. Would she be doing that again today? If she was, it made me wonder once again where they were getting the bodies from. Maybe yesterday was a one off, and it was just bodies that had gathered up over a couple of weeks. That would still be horrific, but slightly less bad.

She hadn't mentioned any of them being rotted or anything though, so I can't imagine it being the truth. Either way, it was dreadful and I really hoped she was not being forced to do the same thing again.

By the time we had finished working, I was once again dead on my feet and found myself stumbling a couple of times whilst walking back to our hut. If this carried on, there was no chance that I could survive. I would not just deteriorate mentally but physically as well.

I still missed my father incredibly. I hadn't gone more than a night without him for nearly ten years and so I just couldn't imagine that I wouldn't see him again any time soon. I wondered why anyone would be so evil that they would split villages, even families up like that and keep us in such dreadful conditions.

I knew it was an Anti-Semitic establishment, but even with such prejudice views against the Jews, I couldn't see the need to keep us living in this hell hole. We were enduring forced labour, probably the main reason we were being kept prisoners in the first place.

The place my father was being kept was filled with the less physically able inmates, I took that as a good sign for them as they didn't have to take part in the backbreaking exertion, so they had more chance of survival. They weren't being worked to the point of exhaustion before being relieved, so I had strong hopes of my father surviving. If one of us to die, I would instantly pick myself over him.

Despite my overtiredness, Stephánia still made her way over to me and invited me back to her hut so that we could catch up on what had happened here so far. She still looked relatively cheerful, a big contrast to my sullen frown, which surprised me. Stephánia had always been a happy person, but I don't know how anyone could keep their composure in a place like this.

She had managed to acquire a bottom bunk bed, unlike me who had been downgraded to a top bunk, and so I could sit on it comfortably whilst Stephánia sat next to me. Although it was still small, when we had our legs crossed we just about fit on.

"Did you have fun popping glass out of specs today?" She inquired sarcastically, starting a conversation up.

As an answer, I held out my hands for her to observe the several gashes covering them. They were relatively painful, but I could block it out with some effort. I was going to have to get used to the pain, I realised. "I think it's pretty self explanatory that I hate glasses."

She chuckled and I probably would have joined in had I had the energy, or found it at all amusing. I did not though and so just sat there continuing to look morbid. "What have you been doing at night then? Anything interesting? The people in here are actually really nice." She informed me, gesturing around at the few other people who hadn't vacated the hut to go somewhere else and were talking in little groups.

I shook my head, but thought back to last night and how I had spent most of it talking to Jakob. That was enlightening and actually rather enjoyable considering the circumstances. I almost wished that I could talk to him tonight as well, but knew it wasn't likely to happen. I should have been grateful to get one conversation out of someone who wasn't Stephánia, not that I disliked her company, and be done with it. I most definitely shouldn't be striving to speak with an SS officer who could point a gun at my head should he have the desire to do so.

"No, I've pretty much slept and worked since I got here. This is the life." I commented sarcastically. There was no point trying to seem happy when I clearly wasn't.

She sighed. "I know that this place is horrible and disgusting and I miss my family, but if I let myself get really depressed about it then I'll lose it. I'll lose all hope that I'm going to see them again and I won't even try to survive in this place." She explained.

"I understand. I do, I just can't do that. I can't pretend to be happy when I'm not. I wish I could, but…" I trailed, failing to really explain what I trying to convey. I wished I could act oblivious and pretend that everything was just fine, but I couldn't. I was too realistic for that. I might not have let any of the grief or misery that was swarming around inside consume me just yet, but I couldn't guarantee that it wasn't going to happen eventually.

"Well, I guess we all cope with things differently." She stated.

I nodded. "Yeah, only you cope with them better than me."

She laughed, but I still couldn't bring myself to join in. "So, have you seen any good looking officers then?" She inquired.

I looked at her incredulously, but couldn't stop my mind slipping back to Jakob again. He was incredibly good looking, right down to his hat which was worn askew on his head. "Are you serious Stephánia?" I cried. "They're keeping us imprisoned in here and your asking if I've been checking them out? One slapped you yesterday morning. Plus they're all sleazy." I ranted, shivering as I remembered the many officer's eyes raking over my slender frame.

She looked slightly taken aback by the venom in my voice as I thought of the soldiers who were holding us hostage. "I know." She admitted. "Besides, I've only really seen one that's worth looking at. He looks about twenty, with brown hair."

I knew instantly that she was talking about Jakob and tried not to show too much recognition. It wasn't that I didn't trust Stephánia, only that she was known for talking about anything to anyone and if I recapped my late night chat, then it would no doubt be around the whole camp before tomorrow. I didn't want to get him into trouble and so I decided to keep that knowledge to myself. "You mean the one who was choosing which line we went it the first day? I guess he was alright, but he's still carrying a gun and probably perfectly willing to point it at our heads." I pointed out.

She nodded. "I know, but you've got to admit that he's handsome."

I grinned, for the first time since I'd arrived here. Jakob was fetching and there was no point trying to deny it. "He is pretty attractive." I agreed.

We both giggled to ourselves which distinctly reminded me of how we used to be. Back in the village, we'd been really good friends and constantly giggling about random things and generally having a good time. We'd spend our days spying on boys around Ajka and laughing gaily as we avoided them narrowly. It was incredible to think just how childish we'd been mere months ago. I'd done a lot of growing up since then, however, and I already knew that if we got out of here alive then nothing would stay the same as it was before.

"Hey, I heard that someone in your hut got put into the line which wasn't dismantling glasses, I wonder what she's spent her days doing. I hope it wasn't something easier than us." She complained.

I opened my mouth, ready to tell her exactly what they had been doing, that it was far from easy, but then closed it again. Stephánia had managed to keep up a cheery persona, managed to avoid the doom and gloom that had already threatened to engulf me. Should I ruin that by telling her about what was really happening here? I might not know any of the details, even who the bodies were, but I knew enough to know that this place was even worse than I could have possibly imagined. I didn't want to bring Stephánia down by making her realise that.

"I don't know. She hasn't really talked about it. She's kept herself to herself really." I lied. I didn't like telling lies to people I liked, but this was for the best. No doubt she would find out eventually, but I was happy for her to retain her innocence for the moment.

She looked disappointed. "That's a shame. I could do with some good gossip around here."

I rolled my eyes at her naivety, but couldn't make another comment because the door burst open and two officers came storming in; one of them I clearly recognised as Jakob. He wasn't as forthcoming as the other one, and maintained the same awkward quality that he always seemed to have when doing anything aggressive.

"Curfew is up! Back to your own buildings, now." The bellicose officer ordered, glaring around the room.

Uncomfortably, I stood up and made my way over to the door where the two soldiers were still stood. I noticed that I was the only one who had moved. I deduced that I must have been the only one who had come to this hut and wasn't sure what I should do.

They were blocking the exit, and I couldn't get past without piping up and requesting that they move. I was far too wary to actually do that and afraid of the consequences though, so I just stuck to standing in the middle of the cramped room, unsure of where I should be putting myself.

Unfortunately, that had gained me some attention and the officer who's identity I was unaware of leered at me. "What are you doing there? Are you going to return to your hut or not?" He demanded, a cold edge to his voice as his eyes raked over my body, stopping on my legs and breasts.

I didn't dare to speak and so I nodded instead, making my way forward and fully prepared for them to just let me past so that I could get back to my own accommodation safely. I didn't make it that far though and the officer grabbed my arm, stopping me in my tracks.

I winced as I tried not to struggle against his vice-like grip. His nails dug into me, no doubt drawing blood, and I flinched, but still didn't try and escape him. I didn't want to provoke him any further. "You didn't answer my question." He snarled.

"Yes." I whimpered.

He dug his nails in deeper and I squeaked in pain against my will. "Look at me when I'm speaking to you."

I tilted my head so that it was now facing him. His face was a picture of anger as I took in his animal like features. His eyes were alight with rage as he kept his hold on my arm. Before I could react, he'd shoved my sideways so that I flew into Jakob.

He instantly helped me up and I stepped away from him. He hadn't even considered the consequences before reaching out to help me and I found that touching. I shouldn't have, though, because the officer also didn't seem to like Jakob's show of slight affection. "Punish her." He instructed him.

Jakob's face was a picture of horror as he looked at the commanding officer. "What? How?" He questioned, still slightly taken aback. I gathered that he hadn't really had to deal with the prisoners in a violent way yet and this was something he especially had wanted to avoid.

"I don't know." He exclaimed, exasperated. "Slap her or something. Just let her know that she needs to realise her place around here."

I gazed up at Jakob, my eyes wide. The pain in my arm was numb as I waited for Jakob to inflict his hand onto my cheek. He caught my eyes and raised his palm, ready to strike my face.

I closed my eyes and waited for the pain to come.

Only it never did. At the last minute, Jakob raised his other hand and slapped that instead of the tender flesh that was my face. The noise of palm hitting palm reverberated around the room and I vaguely heard Stephánia gasp.

The officer obviously hadn't caught that he never really slapped me and I was grateful. I forced tears to prick at the corner of my eyes and instantly raised my own hands to my face, trying to cover up the fact there was no red mark there.

I didn't turn around before mouthing a silent 'thank you' to Jakob, how-ever. I had to at least try and let him know how thankful I was that he'd not hit me. I kept my head down and exited the room, keeping a hold of my cheek as I did so and making sure the officer caught no sight of my unharmed face.

Jakob had just risked an awful lot by not hurting me. If the general had seen his avoidance, then he would have been the one punished. He'd only had to slap me, nothing serious, and I wouldn't have minded if he'd covered his own back by carrying it out. It wouldn't have hurt that much and I didn't want to put Jakob in danger by him treating me too nicely.

As it was, I was still eternally grateful that he'd saved me from further trauma for that night.

AAH, sorry it took my so long to update! It's harder to come up with ideas for this story, because I'm trying to keep it as realistic as possible. I obviously know that there's something's that I'm way off on - such as the hair thing. All the important points I'm trying to keep the same though, I just didn't want her to lose her hair :(

I hope this chapters alright and that I haven't made it too unrealistic!

I think I'm going to write the epilogue now, because I already know how the story will end and I've got a great idea for what I can do for it!

I'll try and update sooner next time! Sorry! Oh, and thanks for all the votes and comments, they're greatly appreciated!

Chapter Six

C hapter Six...

After yet another long day working, I trudged back to my hut. As much as I wanted to go and see Stephánia, I wasn't willing to risk it. I'd put Jakob and myself into a lot of danger by doing that and it wasn't something I wanted to do again.

Stephánia was obviously naïve enough to gamble her safety though, because after laying on the bottom bunk to my bed for a couple of minutes, she came and sat at the side of me. "Are you okay?" She inquired frantically.

She hadn't seen me all day and I could guess that she had been dying to ask that question since yesterday evening. All the pent up worry was making her even more panicky. "I'm fine." I assured her.

"But he slapped you so hard!" She cried, making me wince - hopefully she'd interpret that wince as me recollecting the painful memory, rather than the actual reason.

Jakob hadn't hit me at all, but at least it had been convincing enough so that Stephánia had believed it. "And there was blood running down your arm." She reminded me.

Whereas there was no proof of Jakob's pretend slap, I had a clean wound on my arm where the older soldier had gouged his nails into me. It had bled for a while, but I'd used the thin blanket we had to sleep with to wrap around it until the blood flow stopped. It was beginning to scab up now and wasn't particularly painful anymore, thankfully.

I shook my head. "It wasn't that bad. I had a bit of a red mark before I went to sleep, but that was all. I think it sounded harder than it was." I tried to reason, not being too unrealistic, but I also didn't want to place Jakob in a negative light.

"I didn't think that young officer seemed to bad, but that's definitely persuaded me otherwise. Everyone in this place is evil." She hissed, letting her anger finally show through.

I winced at the bitterness in her voice. It stung to hear her talking about Jakob like that, when really he'd done nothing wrong. He'd protected me, despite knowing what a bad idea that was. It made me guilty to know I was making Stephánia think badly of him because I was shielding her from the truth.

I tried not to sound too lenient when I defended him too her, sounding like I was on his side would only raise unnecessary suspicions. "He didn't really have a choice though, I know I wouldn't want to disobey that man." I held out my arm to remind her. "I know what happens when you don't do exactly what he commands."

Stephánia flinched as she took in the gruesome slice once again. "I suppose. But he wouldn't have taken a job here in the first place if he wasn't prepared to follow orders." She pointed out.

I tried not to scowl, because that would give away how annoyed I was that she was assuming what he was like. Having said that, I presumed that every other soldier in this camp was a crime to humanity until it was proved otherwise. Unlike how it was normally innocent until proven guilty, in this case it was guilty until proved innocent.

"Good point." I agreed through clenched teeth. I was not going to give away how I felt about this and how much more I knew than her, even though I shouldn't. It would just ruin the trust Jakob had seemingly put in me if I broadcast his secrets to probably the loudest mouthed inmate here.

"Have you found out what the other line are doing yet?" She inquired, changing the subject completely. "I'll still be jealous if they're doing something less strenuous than dismantling glasses."

I shook my head grimly. I was keeping more and more secrets lately, and it wasn't a habit I liked to pursue. Lying to people had never been a strong point for me, but when it came to protecting people, I could manage it.

This was one of those occasions.

"How about when we'll see the other side of the camp again?" She queried then, stumping me completely.

I honestly thought she'd have realised we probably wouldn't be seeing them again - at all. I was still coming to terms with that myself. That when I saw my dad may well have been the last time I'd ever see him.

It also came with the knowledge that he would be suffering alone. I'd never been without my dad, since my birth, but whereas I'd only lost him, he'd had to lose my mother too. I knew when she'd died it had been hard on him and he'd only just managed to raise me.

But now he was alone again, he'd gone through the trauma of losing two people now; something I didn't know if I'd be able to bare. This was hard enough.

Hopefully he'd have found someone he knew from the village though. Ajka might be a small town, but if I'd found Stephánia, I couldn't see any reason why he couldn't found someone who he knew too.

Having said that, more people were being chosen to go into his side of the camp, which meant it would be far more crowded and there was less of a chance he would recognise anybody.

"Stephánia…" I trailed off, unsure of how I should approach the subject. She still looked so hopeful, so full of life, despite the horrific situation we'd been placed in. "I…" I had no idea how to break it to her, to make it sound better than the reality was. I didn't think there was any pleasant way of saying that you were never going to see your family again, however.

Stephánia avoided my eyes. "I know." She muttered. "I know I'm being ridiculous. Everyone in here knows the reality. I'm never going to see them again. They're going to work us until we end up like the skeletal forms we saw coming in here, but I have to try. Knowing I'll never see them again is killing me Viktória." She admitted.

I pulled her into a heartfelt hug. Stephánia, with her many family members, was losing so much more than me, and yet she was unbelievably positive. I was still puzzled over what had happened with her two younger sisters, but it was something I would probably never find out.

If the officers here had some fascination with twins, then they had the power and authority to do something about it. Whereas I, who had questions, had no one to ask them too. Even Jakob had been unwilling to answer my queries.

When we leaned back again, I saw the tears streaking down her face. Since I'd said my goodbye to my father, or rather mouthed it, I hadn't shed another tear.

It wasn't that I didn't have things to cry about, because if I wanted, I could probably burst into sobs this instant at the horrendous situation I was in. It was that I didn't want to waste my tears. There was no point in letting myself become more upset than I already was by letting out what I was feeling. By bottling them up and keeping everything contained, I managed to at least keep some kind of composure. It was like a more depressing version of what Stephánia was doing.

We didn't speak, but there wasn't any need to. My hug had shown how much I was offering her support. I didn't mind being her shoulder to lean on when she couldn't stay strong anymore, because I welcomed the comfort just as much.

It was then that I noticed how many people were not returning to our hut. It must be getting to the time when officers began rounding us up and sending up back to our accommodation. I didn't want Stephánia to suffer the same fate that I had yesterday and rushed her to stand up.

"You should get back, people are beginning to move." I pointed out, gesturing around the hut at the number of people who were now gathered here.

Stephánia made the same sweeping gesture that I had and realisation dawned on her face. "You're right, I don't want any injuries tomorrow." She agreed. "I'll see you soon." She vowed, before heading out and back to her own room - if you could even call it that.

I sighed as she exited the building rapidly, avoiding any other moving bodies. Our hut was now full up, but there wasn't a lot of talking going on. Everybody was sat on their allocated beds and appeared deep in thought, just like I probably did. And there was a lot to think about.

It seemed everyone else had come to the conclusion we were stuck here until it came to the worst possible conclusion as well. They knew there wasn't a way out of this, that we were here until we died. That had worsened the mood even more, if that was possible, and even after just a few days, I knew I would be witnessing the breakdowns soon.

The door burst open, similar to how it did yesterday, and I instinctively cowered down in my top bunk which I had retired to. I peered out of the edge, just to see the same two officers. Jakob, and the violent older man.

"Officer Eichel, check that every varmint here is in their correct hut." He instructed, gesturing to Jakob, who he must have been referring to as 'Officer Eichel'.

Tentatively, he stepped further into the cramped room, walking from bunk to bunk and only glancing at everyone. Most people were still on the bottom bunks, and so he had a clear view of the tattoo engraved onto their skin. It was obvious that was what he was checking, since it was our only form of identification.

I was the last bunk, being furthest away from the door, and therefore the last on his travels.

When he reached me, he glanced up and seemed only then to realise I was here. When he was stood at the front, he'd kept his eyes downcast, avoiding looking at anyone - especially his commanding officer.

I was shocked when he reached out and took my arm softly, pulling it down so that he could observe the seven small numbers embellished on my arm.

His hand was smooth as it touched my arm, almost like caress. He didn't handle me with any kind of aggression, like his superior had, and it felt almost soothing. It also made goose bumps litter my skin as I tried to fight the blush which was threatening to surface on my cheeks. I didn't want to look like a silly little girl who found only a slight touch to the arm desirable.

After only a second, he let go. I didn't miss as he turned away from the easily offended soldier at the front as he whispered three simple words to me. "Are you okay?"

The sincerity in his words made me have to smother a smile. Aside from Stephánia, he was the only person who had been even slightly empathetic with me, and I was touched by that.

I gave a subtle nod of the head, assuring him that I was as perfectly fine as I was expected to be, taking the circumstances into consideration. He offered me as much of a smile that he could get away with, before turning around and striding back towards his superior.

He didn't risk a glance back at me, but I could tell by the simple question that he'd asked me that he had at least shown that he cared slightly, because he definitely hadn't given anyone else such presidential treatment - and I'd been observing him extremely closely as he'd been advancing on me.

That wasn't the only thing he'd been treating me with though. When we received rations during work and he was the one handing them out, I'd always be graced with a slightly bigger portion.

Where everyone else would get two mouthfuls of water, I'd been given five. Where everyone else got half a slice of bread, I'd get a full one, with slightly less mould than everyone else's green crumbs.

It was those little things that let me know he cared, at least a little bit. For all I knew, he might be doing exactly the same for other people when he was handing out their rations, but whilst I was still innocent of that knowledge, I wasn't going to question it.

Plus, I found that he was often watching me. When we were working, the soldiers lined themselves up against the wall, so that they had a good view of all the workers. Occasionally, one would move, coming closer and often slapping people if they didn't appear to be dismantling fast enough.

But Jakob never did that. Not that I really expected him too. He seemed so much more passive than everyone else, and I could guess that was because unlike the others, he didn't actually want to be here.

All I could hope, was that they didn't eventually convert him - make him believe that all this was right.

WHOOPS! I didn't realised I'd been so long :S I always hate it when people take this long to update, so I'm pretty sure you're hating me right now :(

Anyway, this chapter isn't even that long :(I hope you still like it though! I've been trying to think of ideas for this, but I've been caught up with my other stories :(

Thankyou! To all the votes and comments though! I'm still slightly amazed everytime I get one :')

Chapter Seven

- -

Chapter Seven...

I muttered a Hungarian curse word under my breath as yet another shard of glass sliced into my delicate hand, allowing a small drop to weep out and onto the floor. My hands were going to be unfit for dismantling these spectacles if I kept being so careless. The only problem was, that we had to be fast, otherwise we'd be punished, but it was impossible to be quick and avoid injury as well.

Glancing around at the officers lined up against the wall, I instantly picked Jakob out among them. His eyes were glazed over as he stared straight forward, avoiding any of us working in front of him. I could guess he didn't want to hurt his eyes with our slowly withering frames and I didn't blame him. None of us were a picture to look at.

A loud cough brought me out of my observations and I turned my attention to the young girl beside me. She seemed to only be sixteen and much frailer than I was. Obviously I was at a marginally better physical standard than the rest thanks to Jakob's extra rations, but this girl appeared to have suffered extensively.

She let out another hoarse bark and I sympathised with her unconditionally, especially when an solder came over.

Instantly, I busied myself with the latest pair of glasses. If I was seen to be slacking off, then I would be punished severely, along with the other few I had witnessed evading their duties. I did let myself witness the interaction out of the corner of my eye, however, unable to deny my curiosity.

"Stop coughing girl." The rough soldier ordered coldly. He was only small, but made up for his lack of height in girth instead, his stomach protruding from his waistline in an unattractive fashion. His face was hard, and it was obvious he was one of the officers who wasn't afraid to take advantage of his power over us inmates.

"Yes sir." The girl whimpered, before erupting into yet another fit of violent coughs and splutters. When she'd finished, a startled look overtook her face, and she fidgeted nervously, knowing that something horrific was about to occur.

And she was right.

In the space of a second, the officer had extended his hand and struck the fragile girl. Not the kind of slap that Stephánia had received, which although hard enough to sting and bruise had not been with full exertion, this blow knock the delicate girl off her feet and left her sprawled across the floor.

I paused, momentarily lifting my head from the glasses I was supposed to be disassembling and waited for her to get up, to move. Only, she never did.

She just lay there, deathly still. He mouth was slightly parted as her cheek rested against the dirty floor. A red mark was clearly visible where the soldier had inflicted his hand on it, and when I glanced up, I noticed that he looked satisfied - almost impressed with himself. I felt like being sick.

He gestured for all the officials to gather round and look. When I took note of Jakob, he was giving off the impression that he really didn't want to go and look, that he knew what was about to happen and was reluctant to witness it.

When he did make his way forward, he chose to stand as close to me as he could get away with. He sent me a comforting glance, but didn't appear too reassured himself. In fact, he looked pale with realisation.

Still not daring to move any closer to the scene, for fear of being harmed myself, I manoeuvred slightly so that I had a better view of what was about to unfold. I knew that it was probably a foolish move of mine, that I didn't actually want to perceive what was happening, but my inquisitiveness got the better of me and I couldn't help myself.

I observed as the man who had slapped her walked forward, holding up her arm and feeling for a pulse. A look of disappointment showed and I felt my heart sink. She must be dead.

"She's alive." He announced, his tone expressing his discontent. Why would he have wanted to kill the poor girl? She was still a child! That in itself proved what kind of monstrosities there were working here, people who would wish to kill.

"What do we do now?" One of the officers who had gather around in-quired. "Take her back to her hut and send her to work again tomorrow?" He suggested.

The officer who had caused this in the first place shook his head, a look of sick pleasure once again took a hold of his face and he walked around the girl's slumped frame. A dark smirk appeared on his face and he waved a hand dismissively to the man's recommendation.

"This girl is far to sick to conduct any more work." He stated, gesturing to her malnourished body. "She's useless now."

"So what do we do with her?" The same officer queried.

In a flash, the man had pulled the gun from his belt and shot the girl in the head. "Sorted." He announced, dismissing the group and walking back to his spot on the wall, allowing the other soldiers to follow him.

I couldn't tear my eyes away though. They were wide and scared as I took in the blood which flowed from her now disfigured head. Being at such a close range had meant the wound was messy, pouring far more blood than I had suspected.

I created a large pool around her and I found tears welling up in my eyes. He'd ended her life, just like that. He'd had no qualms, no consideration for what he'd done, no conscience. He didn't care that she was someone's daughter, possibly someone's sibling. He'd just shot her. Killed her.

And now I'd looked, I couldn't look away. My eyes were fixated on her and I knew I was in a state of shock. The horror I was experiencing was unbelievable, as well as the fear. Yet, even though I knew I was putting myself in more danger by continuing to stare, it wasn't something I could refrain from doing.

Taking one glance away from what was now a corpse, I realised that Jakob was the only other officer still stood standing away from the wall. His expression gave away that he was as aghast as I was, yet was facing the same problem. He just couldn't rip his scrutiny away from her.

When he did the same as me, we shared an appalled look. It told me more than I already knew about how he viewed the treatment of people here. I got the impression that he hadn't witnessed anything so wicked, so despicable, before either and was just as shocked as I was.

Then, he seemed to grasp a hold onto reality and the situation we were actually in. Subtly, he gestured to the glasses in my hand, reminding me what I was actually doing. When I glanced at the other inmates, I spotted that everyone was indeed doing what they were supposed to be, disman-tling glasses at an unbelievable speed. Of course, most of them were pale, shaking and shedding many tears, but they were still doing it. Unlike me.

Tearing my gaze away from the mauled body in front of me and returning my attention to the spectacles in my hand, I tried desperately to continue with my work. Jakob, having been the one to remind me of my duty in the first place, seemed to realise his own then and he returned to his position on the wall.

A considerably paler shade coloured his skin now, however, and I knew that it wasn't only me and the other inmates who'd been affected by this girls death.

What made it even worse, was that I could only refer to her by the number clearly visible on her pale and unmoving arm.

Stephánia shivered with the news that I'd just given. "And he just shot her down?" She clarified.

I shook my head. "No, she was already down. He just finished the job off." I reiterated bitterly.

Stephánia had been in a different hut today, doing the same thing, only at a different venue. That simply proved to me that there were even more deaths here than I originally thought. The sheer number of spectacles in my own building had been enough to horrify me, but another building full of them? That was unbelievable. And who was to say there weren't more? There could be rows of buildings filled with the same amount of glasses, signifying yet more and more deaths.

"I can't believe it." Stephánia repeated what had already been her senti-ments at least three times since the conversation had begun. "And you were right next to her when it happened?" She repeated what I had already told her.

I resisted the sudden urge to roll my eyes at her childish behaviour, but then I realised this was no sort of situation where I could give such a casual gesture. This was serious. More than serious, really. I knew for a fact that this would haunt me, stay with me forever. It was one of those things you can't forget.

"Yes," I whispered, having regained the sense of revulsion and fear that had gripped me when it happened. "I was right next to her."

"This might sound selfish, but I'm glad I wasn't there." She admitted.

I shook my head. "I wish I wasn't there too, but in a way, it's definitely taught me a lesson." I confessed. "It reminded me how much I really don't want to be here, that's for certain."

I wasn't going to explain the many realisations I'd had earlier, because expressing myself wasn't a strong point. I could handle my own thoughts and feelings without having to share them with Stephánia, who was the opposite. She'd always told me how she felt, always confided in me, whereas I bottled it all up.

Stephánia nodded in understanding. "And for that reason, I almost wish I had been there."

It was strange to me, seeing Stephánia being so serious. Back in the village, she'd always been the lively one, the girl who made everyone happy with her bright personality. Even after Adrian's death, she'd managed to bring some light into my life, despite my obvious depression to everyone around me. But now, I could see the effect this was having on her.

I was sure that this was wearing her down and the sullen look that now occupied her eyes was something which had only arrived since we'd been here. I could read the traumatic glances which she occasionally let loose, scanning the area with something that could rival paranoia. She was taking this bad, no matter how much she tried not to show it.

When people began to leave, she left with them, knowing it wasn't good to push her look tonight. Not after the events of the day so far anyway.

I decided it was best for me to go to sleep straight away, to rid myself of the dreadful feeling I'd adopted and get some well needed rest.

Climbing into my bunk, I let myself slip into the depths of sleep.

Startled, I bolted upright. My subconscious had apparently decided that sleep was not an option for me tonight, haunting me with images of the frail girl's lifeless body strewn across the floor and spewing blood for me to see. Like I'd realised earlier, this wasn't something that would leave me quickly, definitely not. This would be plaguing my sleep for a long time.

Unable to lie in my bed any longer, suffocating myself with the low ceiling that was mere inches from my head and the small blanket which still seemed to restrict my movements too much, I climbed down silently. Sneaking away from the sleeping bodies, I slipped out and onto the rickety steps that I'd occupied only a couple of nights previously.

This time, I would be more careful, however. I wouldn't let an officer see me this time, I would run back inside and pretend to be asleep, then if anyone did come to investigate they would never know it was me. My plan was foolproof, or so I assumed.

I let my thoughts drift off, to my father, to the crimes that had been committed today, even to Adrian. Yet none could brighten my mood. In fact, they made it plummet even more. My father, no doubt, would be suffering in the other camp as well. What had happened today couldn't be made better at all, which was obvious before I'd even begun to think about it.

Then there was Adrian. The memories I had with him always made me happier momentarily, whilst I needed a temporary pick up. Today though, today I couldn't even bring up the positive memories. All I could remember was the unbearable grief I had felt after his death. I compared it to the grief I felt now, only to find that it rivalled it well. I was still at a loss to which one effected me most, and I was already sure things could only get worse for me here.

Being so distracted by my thoughts, I hadn't even noticed the approaching figure, a grave mistake. Jumping up, alarmed, I made an attempt at scurrying back inside. Just as I was about to snatch the door and open it, the soldier beat me to it, grabbing my arm and turning me around.

The hold wasn't possessive; it wasn't hurtful or angry. Because of that, I could guess it was Jakob who had found me.

When he did spin me around, I found myself much closer to him than I'd expected. He was towering above me, but not in an unpleasant way; more that I felt safe with him - a foolish mistake as far as I was concerned. I couldn't help it though.

My nose was practically touching his chest, so when I lifted my head and peered up timidly, I was a lot closer to his face than I'd anticipated, not that I was complaining particularly. His soft eyes brought back the memory of the girl being shot today, how he'd looked just as sickened as I did.

And for the first time since the morning's events, I let a tear slip from my eye. Even when it had happened I'd been too shocked to let myself grieve for this girl who's identity I didn't even know, but now I could let it out, hopefully to an understanding Jakob.

Hesitantly, he raised a hand and brushed away the stray tear from my face, leaving slight tingles from where he'd touched my skin. It served the opposite purpose to what he'd intended though, because I burst into full blown tears now.

As an automatic reaction, I took a step forward and buried my head into his chest, winding m arms around his torso as I tried to muffle the sobs escaping my mouth for risk of being detected. He froze, for a second, clearly taken aback by my bold actions, but then he seemed to realise what he was supposed to do and reciprocated my hug, letting his hands rest on my waist securely.

I sought his comfort and after what felt like forever, I managed to pull back awkwardly. That was completely inappropriate of me, but in the spur of the moment I hadn't been able to resist. I'd needed him to reassure me, even if it was only through him holding me gently like he had done.

"Sorry," I muttered embarrassedly.

He shook his head, a small smile on his face. "It's okay. I think I needed that too." He admitted. It was only then that I noticed the still haunted look on his face. He obviously couldn't get the image of the girl from his head either.

He took a step away from me, but only to take a seat on the stairs we'd occupied together those few nights ago. Without him even having to gesture, I took my place next to him. We sat in a comfortable silence for many minutes, just pondering over our thoughts, because there were lots of them to mull over.

When someone did speak, it was him who broke the silence. "I'm sorry you had to see that this morning." He apologised, as if it was somehow his fault that I'd witnessed the crime against humanity.

"There was nothing you could do about it, besides, you didn't want to see it was much as I didn't want to see it, so I could be saying the same to you." I replied.

There was a small quirk of his lips, which told me he'd been impressed by my reasoning. His posture was more relaxed now, and he sat slumped forward slightly, unlike how he was in the day time, with his back straight and taught to attention. His cap, however, was still slightly askew in his trademark position, just revealing a wisp of brown hair from underneath it.

"How do you think my father if fairing?" I inquired suddenly. My thoughts had been on him for most of the day and this might be my only opportunity to get any sort of truth from someone. I might not like it, but I still wanted it.

An awkward, guilty look passed over Jakob's face and I knew what it meant - that it was bad. "Viktória..." He trailed off, momentarily diverting my attention from the mission at hand. Somehow, the way he said my name managed to illicit feelings of warmth inside me. His German accent, although I should hate it, only served to further how great my name sounded on his tongue. "I don't know if I can tell you the truth." He admitted.

I paused. Well then I needed to convince him that I could. "Why?" I prompted him to continue, to at least disclose some snippet of information to me.

"Because I don't want to hurt you."

As much as that touched me, it wasn't a good enough answer. "I'm hurting from not knowing the truth; from worrying about him every minute of every day. Just tell me, please." I begged, praying for him to understand, to grasp how important this was to me.

He muttered something under his breath in his native tongue, so that it was incomprehensible to me. Suddenly, he grasped my hand. "Viktória," he whispered my name again. "You're right, you do deserve the truth." He conceded. "But, you can't tell anyone else." He set me with an intense gaze. I opened my mouth to ask if I could tell Stephánia, but he spoke over me. "No one." He reiterated. "If people found out, I'll be killed for having told you."

That definitely put it into perspective for me and I blanched. I didn't want to be responsible for Jakob's death under any circumstances. "I won't tell anyone." I vowed sincerely. It looks like this would be more information I was keeping to myself.

"Your father, is, dead." He stated blatantly, his eyes betraying how much he hated to say that.

The shock of this revelation hit me hard, and had I been standing, I would have staggered backward as though he'd struck me. Dead? No. Never. I couldn't bring myself to believe it. I'd been convincing myself that I wanted to know the truth, but this had changed my mind completely. I'd rather live in ignorant bliss than with the knowledge that my father was no longer in the world of the living.

Jakob reached out, offering a sincere gesture of support, but I fixed him with a cold glare. "Don't touch me." I ordered, pulling away from him.

It wasn't that I blamed Jakob, just that I needed to refrain from losing my composure and giving in to the support that he offered. I should stay strong and get what I really want to know from him. The hurt look on his face did make me feel relatively guilty though.

"How did he die?" I choked out, ignoring his wounded face as much as I could.

Jakob sighed and averted his eyes. "He was gassed, along with everyone else who goes into the same line as he did." He explained.

My shock became even more evident then, as I took in the bigger picture. This wasn't just my dad, this was hundreds, thousands even, of people being slaughtered because of some extreme racist views. "Everyone." I repeated. And to think I'd wanted to be in that line as well.

In a way, I still did. Then, I wouldn't have to deal with any of this. I wouldn't have had to acknowledge my father's death. I wouldn't have had to suffer through malnutrition and dehydration, witness the atrocious deeds here, just to die at the end of it anyway. It would have been so much easier.

"I'm sorry." Jakob stated, his eyes themselves expressing how genuine he was being. I couldn't accept it yet though, I had to carry on pushing.

"Would it have been painless? Or would he have suffered?" I urged him to tell me more.

This was the main question I wanted answered. If it had been painless, if he hadn't suffered, I would be able to accept it. Acknowledge that it had been for the best. That if he had survived then he would have suffered, whereas a painless death would have been insignificant for him - he wouldn't have even felt it.

I saw the indecision on Jakob's face then and I knew what the answer was before he even said it. He'd been considering whether or not to lie and save my feelings, but in the end, he did as I wanted and gave me the truth. "It would have been unbearable." He informed me ruefully. "It takes about twenty minutes to die in the chambers and their skin would be red, yellow even green. Many people foamed around the mouth and bled from their ears. I can't even imagine-" He stopped, unable to finish.

This time, I couldn't keep the tragic sobs escaping my throat. My façade slipped completely and I broke down so that I was practically immobile on the floor. Hesitantly, Jakob patted my back, but it did nothing to help me.

I was overcome with grief and it only intensified when I realised the same had happened to Stephánia's parents, to everyone's family who had managed to survive this long. It was horrendous.

"I'm so sorry." Jakob whispered sincerely.

I managed just about to gain enough composure to tell him that it wasn't his fault, because it wasn't. He'd just been the messenger, there was nothing he could do about that. I'd asked him to tell me. "Thanks for telling me the truth."

He looked at me as though I was crazy. "Why would you want to know that?" He asked incredulously.

"Because now I know. Sure, it may have darkened my outlook on life even more, but I know for definite now. There's no more deliberation." I tried to rationalize.

A look of understanding crossed Jakob's face. "I was the same with my dad. In a way, I was horrified when I found out exactly what they'd done to him, but at least I knew. It stopped me wondering for hours on end what he'd been through."

It was strange how we'd actually felt the same emotions. Jakob could empathise with me, because he'd been there, done that. He'd lost his father to the monstrosities that went on here too, it was probably even worse hearing that though, because Jakob's father had been tortured, suffered much more than mine had.

I wiped my eyes quickly, trying to eradicate the tear stains that now covered my face. "I'm sorry about what happened to your father." I told him seriously. Nobody deserved to suffer that fate, especially for doing nothing wrong, but trying to stick up what was right.

When I died, I wanted it to be for a cause so noble as well, but stuck in this hell hole, I knew it would a pointless death that I was served.

Sorry it took me so long to update again :(But, it is longer this time! I hope this wasn't too gloomy, with the main topic being death and all, but I'm trying to keep it realistic and people would have been falling down dead all over the place, so I thought I'd put in a scene explaining that and making the officers look even worse. But, it had lots of Jakob in!

I know people leave it way longer than this to upload, but I always try to be efficient!

Hope you enjoy this, and thanks for voting and commenting on this story!

Chapter Eight

C hapter Eight...

Trying not to appear ridiculously guilty when denying any sort of knowledge to Stephánia's questions was getting harder and harder.

"I just want to know what happened to my parents." She complained, a slight hint of desperation making itself known in her voice.

I knew how she was feeling, down to the last emotion. She was scared, depressed and angry. I'd been there, known what it felt like wondering where you're family were and what was happening to them, although I'd found out now.

Like when I'd held back the knowledge of what the girl hauling bodies was spending her time doing, I was also restricting this information for a reason, other than the fact Jakob had made me vow not to tell anyone.

Stephánia, despite her weaknesses now shining through marginally, was doing a lot better at staying positive than I was. She was still optimistic, still trying to make the best of an unbearable situation.

This knowledge, would be the last straw for her. Knowing that she'd lost her parents, lost them forever, would push her to losing the sanguine mentality she'd adopted, and I didn't want that for her.

As well as the obvious reason that I didn't want her to suffer anymore than she had too, because I was her friend and I wouldn't want that for her - or anyone for that matter. No, I also had selfish grounds for wanting her to stay mentally stable.

Stephánia was one of only two things keeping me sane here. Having her to talk to, to trust, was keeping me just about balanced. She was there when I needed to complain, to express my hatred of the many people here. Without that, I would let even more detest build up inside me, until it pushed me over the edge as well. Without Stephánia's support, I knew that I wouldn't be able to cope either.

Jakob, sure, he was helping me out too, but that wasn't enough. I saw him very rarely, and even that was a big risk. I couldn't quite bring myself to be completely honest with him, because although I did trust him, I couldn't guarantee anything here; which was understandable.

No, I needed Stephánia here to keep my upright.

"I wish I knew." I answered her grievance with as nostalgically as possible. I also tried to conceal the flair of pain that built up inside me. I knew exactly where my father was. He was a pile of ashes scattered in some forgotten place, along with thousands of others. He was one of many who had been murdered unnecessarily, killed for no purpose whatsoever.

"And I'm still curious what happened to the twins, that was really strange." She commented, a thoughtful, but still indignant, look on her face.

To that question, I really didn't have to hide my knowledge, because I didn't have any. I could definitely agree that it was strange, however. I somehow doubted that anyone would be getting presidential treatment here, yet that appeared to be the case. "I've no idea."

I couldn't think of any reason why the twins would need to be taken away separately, if they were only going to be killed anyway. Surely then they would have just been put in the line to be gassed if that was the case.

No, even I could realise that there was something odd going on there. There was something that these officers had either for or against twins. It was something I'd have to consult Jakob with. If I could get information off anyone around here then it would be him.

Not that I was sure I actually wanted to know what was going on with them, no doubt it would be just as bad as what had happened to my father, or worse, if that was even possible.

"Did anything abnormal happen whilst you were working today?" She changed the line of conversation completely. It had been two days since the girl was shot down mercilessly, but nothing interesting had happened in them so far.

Today, it had been exactly the same again. Jakob was supervising us again today, as well as handing out rations. I presumed he was left to do that because he wasn't as high a ranking as the others, being forced into this rather than having a choice like the rest of them.

He'd, like normal, given me a considerably bigger portion of everything, which I'd had to conceal from everyone else. Whilst everyone else was already beginning to ware away, I was still only marginally more malnourished than I was when I arrived here.

"Nope, everything was like it's supposed to be today." I informed Stephánia grimly. Although I would never wish for anyone's death, it still felt wrong to say that it was how it should be. None of this should ever be happening. It was all wrong.

The scuffling of people hurrying back to their own huts caught my attention then and I sent a panicked look to Stephánia. "Come on, you need to head back." I told her in a rushed voice, gesturing for the door, half expecting someone to burst through it and punish us.

My expectations weren't too far off, however, when Jakob opened the door softly. Unlike normal, he was alone today, so there was no aggression to be seen in both his expression or actions.

We locked eyes in an instant, causing a shiver of something I couldn't quite identify to spread up my spine. After sending me an almost identifiable smile, he turned his eyes from me, so as not to raise attention to myself.

"Is everyone back to their huts?" He checked, his German accent wrapping around me as it coloured his words. It was something that I found oddly attractive. It complimented his deep, almost gruff, voice.

I pushed Stephánia, who was looking beyond nervous, up and gestured for her to go back to her own accommodation.

I could understand why Stephánia was terrified, though. Last time this had happened, I had received a 'slap' off Jakob, so now Stephánia believed that he wasn't afraid to hurt any of us.

I, however, knew otherwise, and so I wasn't afraid to get Stephánia to move. She just needed to get back before anyone else came in and really did hurt her.

Jakob took in her frail form moving towards him and then scurrying out through the door. She didn't even look back, which I didn't blame her for. I'd have been running as fast as possible as well.

I found it rather amusing, how when Stephánia had made it out unharmed, that several more people also found the courage to move and head back to their own huts then as well. I wry smile appeared on my face, as I found myself trying not to let a small chuckle escape.

Jakob caught my eye and also my amusement, letting a small smile slip onto his own face. "I just need to come round and inspect the bunks." He informed us, before making a move forward.

Peering quickly over every top and bottom bunk, he soon reached my own. Unlike with everyone else, he came much closer to me and had a much more observant look, only not at the bed, but at me.

"Are you okay?" He whispered almost incoherently.

I managed a small nod, not wanting to alert any attention to myself by accidentally speaking too loud.

"Good," Jakob announced, still barely loud enough for me to hear. "Well, sweet dreams, Viktória."

I felt the same shivers as he said my name, but tried not react on it, just giving him a sweet smile and reminding him that he should really be moving by now, having already spent at least double the time here than everywhere else.

We shared one more small twisting of lips, but then he had gone again, vacating the hut and no doubt moving onto the next one.

Sighing, I lay back down in my bed. I just needed to do as he'd advised now, and have some sweet dreams.

In this hell hole, though, I didn't think that was going to be very achievable.

"Can I ask you something?" I directed my question at Jakob, as we sat next to each other in front of my hut. These late night meeting had become sort of habit it for us, as well as becoming one of the few refuges from the horror of what went on during the day.

Jakob, once again, looked hesitant, which I could understand. "I guess." He conceded reluctantly. I knew he was expecting me to ask something he wasn't supposed to answer, or something he didn't feel comfortable answering. And he was right to think that, because I wasn't asking a conventional question.

"Why do people here have such an interest in twins?" I dared to inquire. In a way, I almost wasn't expecting an answer. He'd been hesitant to tell me about my father, but had given in eventually, just because it was directly related to me. This, however, wasn't about me. This was about Stephánia. I owed her to find out, even if I didn't tell her the exact truth to start off with.

He paused then, but unlike the knowing, yet tentative, look I received last time, this one was filled with pure puzzlement. "I, have no idea." He admitted, and somehow, I knew that he was telling the truth.

I raised an eyebrow slightly. "No clues whatsoever?" I checked. Surely, he had to know something. He couldn't be completely oblivious to something that was going on here, even if he only knew a few details about it.

He thought about it, then shook his head in denial. "No." He reiterated. "The senior officials, the guys that are really in charge, they always tell us to look out for twins. That if we get a pair, then we'll get rewarded. Only, they've never really explained why, why they had this obsession with twins. Obviously no one dared to be inquisitive, because you're more likely to be given punishment than a bonus in this place."

I sighed, tapping my fingers lightly against my face. There was something really strange going on there. "That's not right." I mused aloud. "There's something really not right about that, and that's saying something considering where we are."

Jakob nodded. "You know, I've never actually considered it before." He admitted. "That makes me feel even worse. It's only happened once, seeing twins, two girls, they looked about twelve, thirteen?"

I grimaced, instantly realising who they were. "Twelve." I filled in glumly. So Jakob had been the one that sent Stephánia's sisters to the unknown that was what happened to twins.

Jakob raised an eyebrow. "You knew them?" He inquired, appearing even more guilty now.

"Stephánia's sisters." I explained briefly.

"I'm sorry." It seemed like he was saying that to me a lot lately. I wasn't sure how much I liked it. I didn't want his apologies, or his sympathy, because although I knew he was partly to blame for all that was happening here, he was a victim too. He might not have to be here, torturing people both mentally and physically, but I knew he was suffering too.

I waved him off, trying to stay strong. "What happened to them?" I inquired, requesting for him to carry on the tale he had been reciting.

"My colleague, I can't even recall his name, went to fetch someone, and then the twins were taken away. I didn't see where they were led, but it was definitely not into either sides of the camp - concentration or extermination."

Although I had never heard the terms used to precisely, I could guess that this side was concentration, and my father's side had been extermination; since that was the perfect way to describe his death. It hadn't been a mercy killing, there hadn't been any sort of justification in the way he was murdered. It was pure extermination.

"So, there's no way of finding out about them then." I figured out, slightly disheartened by that. But, at least I could say I'd tried now. I'd done all that I could, even if it was minimal. That made me feel better.

Jakob nodded his head, still looking as though the blame was going inwards. "Unless, I could try and snoop around, see what I can gather. There's tons of rooms I've never even ventured towards before, I'm sure I could take an adventure around them." He offered gallantly.

I shook my head instantly, though. "No, you can't risk that." I objected. "You've put yourself at enough risk for me as it is, that's pushing it too far. If you got into trouble for it because of me, I wouldn't be able to forgive myself." I admitted honestly.

Jakob regarded me closely. "You shouldn't even care about what happens to me." He pointed out, still observing me with curious eyes.

Unable to uphold the eye contact, I averted my own, unwilling to face the truth that was brewing inside me. "You've risked so much for me." I informed him. "You've helped me so much since I've been here, I couldn't possibly want anything to happen to you now."

I felt the heat rise to my cheeks as I expressed something I had only ever thought mentally. Despite not even describing the half of my emotions, it was more than I even planned on sharing. Jakob had helped me immensely though and it was only natural that I'd feel something towards him now. No one could acquire such kindness from a person and be expected to hate them, it just doesn't work that way.

Jakob's gaze wasn't inquisitive anymore when I glanced back up at him this time, it had gained a tender quality now, as they shone with something I couldn't quite identify.

"I don't want to get hurt either, but for a good cause like this, or you, I'd definitely be more willing." He confessed, a small smile conveying how genuine that statement actually was.

I was still confused as to why Jakob had taken any particular interest in me in the first place, but I couldn't say that I was complaining. Anyone was lucky to have him looking out for them here, him and Stephánia were the only things that could possibly brighten my day.

The amount of honesty in our conversation was slightly unnerving, but I found myself unable to tear my gaze away from his own. It held so much emotion that I wasn't sure if I'd ever seen something so sincere.

The only other time I'd seen a look packed full with genuine feelings, was when Adrian had been on his deathbed.

He lay, obviously in his last moments, and then grabbed my hand. We were completely alone and he just gazed at me, his face contorted slightly with pain.

Then, he broke the silence with three words I'd never expected to hear from him. "I love you." He whispered, almost incoherently, before coughing violently and grimacing in what I can only assume was unbelievable agony.

I had obviously never heard the words spoken to me before, except from my father, who'd meant it from the point of view of a parent, rather than Adrian, who was clearly meaning it in a different way.

He wheezed once again, bringing me back to the reality that these were his final moments. Of course he'd choose now to confess that to me. When I had no time to think of a rational response.

I was left unable to think of a reply, but as he lay there, looking at me so filled with hope, I just smiled and tried to look as passionate as he did. "I love you too." I lied, feeling the tears washing down my face then.

It wasn't that I didn't loved him, because I did. I loved him as my best friend. As the person who was always there for me. But I wasn't in love with him like he was me. I couldn't tell him that though, not when he was about to lose his life at such an early age.

No, it was better to lie, to make him feel better, at least whilst he was still living. Although lying to him still made me feel guilty, telling him that I didn't love him would have killed me. I couldn't have lived with myself, knowing that I'd crushed him like that mere minutes before he passed away.

When I uttered the words back to him, his whole face brightened, acquiring such an expression of relief and joy that it reinforced my decision. Telling him of my non-existent feelings was definitely the right thing to do.

Then, his face dimmed again, and he collapsed backwards into another spluttering fit. Only when this one had finished, he didn't squeeze my hand to let me know that he was okay. He didn't offer me a small smile, filled with pain, but happiness at the same time. There was nothing. Only his calm face, tranquil as it didn't twitch in the slightest.

He was gone.

Coming back to reality, I felt the wetness now around my eyes. I always refrained from bringing up that memory for this precise reason - it made me cry every time.

I missed Adrian all the time, but I'm glad he wasn't still alive to be enduring this place. His strength and youth would have assured him a place on this side of the camp, which meant he would still be alive now, but instead of dismantling glasses like me, I could guarantee that he would have been hauling dead bodies. Not something I would wish on anyone; except maybe the atrocious people who were enforcing it on us.

A soft hand resting itself on my shoulder broke me out of the thoughts I was currently engrossed in. Once I got thinking of Adrian, it was hard for me to tear myself away. He was such a delicate topic for me.

"Are you okay?" Jakob inquired gently, extending his arm a step further and wiping the tears which had escaped my, probably red, eyes with his thumb.

"I was just thinking about someone I used to know." I explained, trying not to let my voice quiver like it so desperately wanted to. I didn't like showing weakness in front of people, and Adrian was definitely a weakness of mine.

"Do you want to talk about it?" He wasn't prying, just offering some support. He didn't know what to do to help me unless I told him what I was thinking.

Our declarations of feelings long forgotten now, I found that maybe I did want to tell him. Considering the precarious situation, it wasn't likely that I would be around for much longer. Who would I tell about Adrian when I was gone? No one would know just how highly I had thought of him, I should just tell Jakob so that I'd told someone.

"His name was Adrian." I began, still trying to calm my voice so as not to let it give away how upset I got when I was thinking about him. "We were best friends since we were really little, we were engaged and everything." I smiled slightly at that. When Adrian had said those three little words to me, I knew he'd been more than happy about our marriage arrangement. "When I was fifteen, he contracted typhoid and died." I ended the story bluntly.

Jakob's face softened even more and he looked at me sympathetically. He didn't apologise to me, like he had when I mentioned people who had been harmed within the walls of this place, because he didn't feel at all to blame for this; it was pure unlucky coincidence.

Instead, the hold his hand had on my shoulder intensified, as if he was spreading his support through the small amount of contact. "I hate how you've had to go through so much." He muttered almost silently. "You don't deserve any of it."

I couldn't help the slight smile that graced my lips with that. No one had even empathised with me so much before, because he'd been through the same loss as me, he suffered every day as well.

"You don't deserve all the misery you go through either." I replied genuinely.

"I do. I'm a coward."

I sighed, if he could never forgive himself for working here, then I don't know how he'll ever move on. "You can't keep feeling guilty." I informed him exasperatedly. "I already said that I would have done the same, so doesn't that mean that I do deserve all this after all?" I pointed out, trying to make him see what I was seeing.

He paused then, presumably thinking of an contradiction to my well argued point. "But," He began, before stopping again, stumped.

"But nothing." I replied. "It's not your fault about what happened to your father and none of this," I gestured around me at the surrounding buildings, "is you fault either. You aren't to blame for any of the destruction here."

"I don't know how you worked that out." He told me, disbelievingly. "Don't you blame me, at all, for any of this? Don't forget I'm the one who put you into this place. Shouldn't you be cursing me right now and hoping for something horrible to happen to me?"

He just wasn't grasping what I was saying! I wasn't blaming him, I couldn't. "If you were really bad, then you wouldn't be sitting here with me right now, having a normal conversation, sympathising with me because my best friend died two years ago. You wouldn't be slipping me extra rations. And, you would have slapped me when you were told to." The last one really hit the nail on the head and I knew he couldn't get out of admitting what he'd done was good, not bad.

Jakob removed the hat which was sat askew on his head, revealing rather short brown hair, which he promptly ran his hand through. It was strange how much different he looked without the hat one, and how attractive he looked both ways.

"I suppose." He admitted, dragging my attention away from his undeniable good looks and back to him.

I smiled widely. "Good, well at least you know that I don't blame you for all of this." I assured him for good measure.

"You don't realise how much it means to hear you say that." He told me, a small smile now also occupying his own lips. "Also, I'd appreciate it if you didn't tell anyone that I give you more food and water than everyone else."

I looked at him as though he was crazy. "Of course I wouldn't. I know how much trouble you'd get into for that."

He shook his head. "I wouldn't get into trouble for it." He revealed, confusing me immensely.

"Why not? I thought the whole point of this place was that you worked us until we died." There was no point in trying to soften up the truth. That was what they were doing. "Why would be let off for keeping me more alive than everyone else?"

"Because nearly all the officers do it." He explained, puzzling me further. These officers all seemed like brutes, why would they be attempting to save someone's life. "It's not that I would get punished for this, it's what I'd have to claim I was doing."

My eyebrows knitted together. I knew that Jakob was avoiding spilling it to me, but I was going to get it out of him, so he might as well get it over and done with.

"The soldiers, they all have their favourites." He began, his face growing dark with anger. "They keep them alive, but it's not out of kindness, it's because they like to have the same one every time." I was still slightly puzzled, but I got the general idea. Jakob saw that I wasn't completely with it though, and so he just stated it bluntly. "They rape them."

I gasped, unable to keep it in. I shouldn't have been particularly surprised considering how many other atrocious deeds were carried out around here, it was just I hadn't even suspected the possibility of it. Rape? It was unheard of to me. Almost like a legend, a myth, because it would have never happened in Ajka.

"I can't believe it." I breathed almost incomprehensibly. "You'd have to say you were raping me if someone found out?"

Jakob averted his eyes, but nodded. "And I don't know if I could do that. When one person is known to be targeted, the other officers will start to pick on her too. I couldn't have that done to you." He explained.

I shook my head, not quite appreciating what he was saying to me because I was still failing to grasp the situation in the first place.

"Do you know of anyone who's being targeted at the moment?" I inquired, unable to help myself. It could be someone in my hut, and I wouldn't have even considered it.

"No," he admitted. "No one near here, but you can normally pick them out anyway, just because they've not lost enough weight."

"Who's still looking rather the brawny then?"

"Actually, that girl you were sitting with earlier, Stephánia is it? She's looking quite well off considering how long you've been going without enough food already."

I felt my breathing stop completely. "You think that Stephánia's being raped?" I shuddered at the thought of someone taking advantage of such a sweet girl. Stephánia didn't deserve anything like that, that was for certain.

Then I thought of her still positive attitude. No, no one could be doing such a horrific thing to her with her still being to unbelievably optimistic. It must just be coincidence that she wasn't quite looking as malnourished as she should have been by now.

I answered my own question for Jakob. "No, she isn't. Stephánia couldn't still be going so strong if she was being abused like that. I know it." I knew that I was assuring myself more than him, but I couldn't accept something so disgusting was happening and I wasn't doing anything about it.

Jakob shook his head at my dismissal of his observations. "I agree, it must just be that she hasn't been affected by the lack of food quite yet."

I nodded vehemently. Nothing was happening to Stephánia, it couldn't be.

Ah! Super long chapter! And I even updated sooner than normal! Also, THIS STORY GOT ONTO THE WHAT'S HOT LIST. :O :D :O :D It was only for a couple of days and really low down, but :O it was definitely on there ;) Thanks to all the votes and comments that put it there! It actually made my day!

I hope this chapter, and all the stuff at the end about the rape and stuff wasn't too harsh and stuff, but it definitely would have happened, maybe not exactly the same, but still there. I don't want to make this too dark and stuff, but it needed to happen to fall in with my plot :)

I hope you enjoy it! And please vote and comment :')

Chapter Nine

Chapter Nine...

The distant sound of shouting, gunfire and screams of agony shook me from my sleep that night. I'd only just managed to drift off, after processing the shocking news that Jakob had given me, suggesting the Stephánia might possibly be being abused in such as way.

That flew straight from my mind, however, when the door burst open. Glancing around, most people had already been woken up by the unknown commotion anyway, but the remaining few who were still sleeping soundly were now wide awake and sat up.

I think people slept with one eye open in this place, which is understandable, considering the circumstances.

Ironically, it was Jakob who was now standing in the doorway, his stance considerably more aggressive than normal. That shocked me so much that I felt the hairs stand up on the back of my neck. If something was so important that Jakob could become so riled up, then it must be worth fearing.

"Everybody up, now." He ordered, his strong voice carrying across the small room.

Instantly, there was upheaval as people rushed around manically, climbing down from their top bunks and scrabbling around, attempting to get in some kind of order for fear of being punished by the surprisingly bellicose looking Jakob in the doorway.

Despite knowing the danger that surrounded my thoughts, I couldn't help but admire his figure from the back of the now single file queue. Everything had gone silent as we waited for further instructions, but it just gave me more time to appreciate his appearance.

His aggressive stature expressed an air of danger that I found oddly appealing. It made him look even more manly than normal and the intense glint in his eyes made my insides oddly warm and my chest constrict.

Averting my eyes, I listened as he barked out a couple more orders, his German accent more predominant in his aggravation. "Follow me."

Some people were shaking with apprehension, obviously assuming that something bad was going to happen. I joined them in the belief it would be a terrible event, but I didn't bother with the shaking part. If something ruthless was about to occur, I was already prepared. I'd been expecting something horrific to happen to me since the minute I walked through here. It had just got worse with the more and more knowledge that I gained.

Others appeared to have the same reaction as me, keeping a straight face and the panic concealed behind their eyes. My thoughts went out to Stephánia, how was she fairing up? Because from the amount of noise that I could now here, it wasn't just our hut which had been intruded upon.

Walking outside, I was met by an overwhelming number of people, only they weren't milling around, like you'd expect of such a large crowd. Instead, they were all organised into their respective hut-mates, just like we were, with an officer heading their line.

Then, line-by-line, we were led around the many huts. The further we went, the more riotous the shouting became, the louder and more striking the sound of gunshot became. Glancing around anxiously, I wasn't sure what to expect.

Aside from knowing it was the German's doing the firing and no doubt shooting at the Jews, I had no clue as to why they were being shot or what the consequences would be.

I did know that was where we were heading, however. Had they decided to just massacre us all suddenly? Had we served our purpose now? Become too weak? Or were they giving us a warning? Showing us what would happen if we weren't careful and shooting the people who had already been here too long. I didn't know, and to be honest, I don't think I wanted to know.

The scene that played about before me after we rounded the next corner, left me speechless in itself. People, were everywhere. All men, half were clad in crisp uniforms, donning the SS logo, the other half wearing ragged shorts and t-shirts that barely covered them.

The gunshots could now be seen as well as heard as the German men fired round upon round into the mass of Jewish men, all at the ripe age we were. I still wasn't sure why, but knew instantly it was unfair and cruel, without an explanation.

Dying to run to the front, ask Jakob for answers, anything, I held myself back. I didn't want to end up the one with a bullet through my skull.

Observing the commotion in front of me once again, I tried to get an understanding of the situation. Unlike when I had first looked and thought the officers were just firing into a crowd, it was actually much the opposite.

The men were fighting, for their lives, launching themselves at officers, throttling them and trying to cut off their air, whilst shielding their bodies, some even trying to break necks. The soldiers were stopping them, shooting endless rounds at their aggressive postures, but missing many times thanks to a combination of their bad aims and how fast their targets were manoeuvring themselves.

We were lined up, so that we could witness the horror easily. Being one of the closer huts to the disturbance meant that we were lined up at the front, giving me front row seats to the massacre. Jakob, who was still at the front of our hut's group, chose to stand directly in front of me.

He made eye contact with me and even though his look was trying to be reassuring, I could still see the anger in it; the same anger he had demonstrated when barging into our room earlier. I wasn't sure of the cause for that anger yet, but I was going to try and piece it together when I found out some more information on the situation.

By the way he stood, so close to me that his back blocked most of the scene, I could tell he was trying to save me the horror of watching such atrocities. It wasn't working very effectively, however, and I still caught the glimpses of blood and guts washing about the grey floor.

Instead of being squeamish by the dead bodies, the various limbs that seemed scattered across the ground, I was more aghast at the amount of death there; at how many people, both SS and Jewish, had been slaughtered. Obviously I couldn't bring myself to be sympathetic towards the soldiers, but it didn't mean that I would ever wish for their deaths. It still made me feel uneasy to know that so many people had lost their lives in such a small period of time.

Looking either side of me now and searching through the crowd, seeing if I could pinpoint Stephánia, I found myself unable to. She must be lost in the sea of other girls also being crowded together to observe the butchery.

Hopefully she would be further back, without a clear view of what was happening. It might be enough to finally break her optimistic outlook if she witnessed the extent of this.

A man's voice brought me out of my search through the crowd and back to the scene in front of me. Now few men left, they were all lined up, facing us. With two officers to every man, they had no chance of escaping - even with the amount of struggling they were doing. They were expecting death, if not punishment before hand, so I could understand their desperate resistance towards the people restraining them.

One man now stood had the front, pacing up and down, swirling a gun around his finger in a smug fashion. They way he stood so proudly made my lip curl in disgust. No one should be able to feel pride in achieving all that murder.

He sneered at the many people stood in front of him, leering at a couple of the girls nearer to the front. In that moment, I recognised him as the same man who had slapped Stephánia only the first morning we'd been here. His stout figure, with the same malicious glow in his eyes, was unforgettable and I wasn't surprised that he had been the one leading such horrendous events.

"These people," he gestured at the line of trembling men behind him, and then at the corpses which littered the floor. His voice carried out to the back of the crowds and was far louder than I had expected. "Thought that it would be a good idea to hold a rebellion, commit mutiny." His quote marks around the word mutiny were accompanied with a smirk and a couple of short, humourless laughs from the men behind him. Even on their deathbeds he was making a point of mocking them.

"And, we've pulled you out here, so you can see why we wouldn't recommend it."

In a flash, he had whirled around, shooting one of the men in the head, so that he collapsed lifelessly to the ground, blood forming an increasingly large pool around him. The two soldiers who had been confining him took a step back, but there was no disgust on their faces, only grim satisfaction.

The officer also showed a glint of manic pleasure as he studied the now lifeless body. "All these men are going to die." There was no sympathy or concern in his voice as he spoke the statement, only anticipation of the cold murder he was about to commit.

Another gun was fired and I heard a man groan in pain. Taking a peek around Jakob's shoulder, which was still partially blocking my view, I saw a man grabbing his arm in agony. The two officials that had been restraining him had also taken a step away, so that the man could be fired on at will.

"Only some, will have a much more painful death." The bitter officer at the front sneered, before letting off two more shots, getting the man in one foot and the leg. Both places wouldn't kill him instantly, but would let him endure the pain for a much longer period, as he bled to death slowly.

As if actions such as homicide weren't bad enough, purposely torturing someone was simply preposterous and evil - pure evil.

I heard the thud as the man collapsed, still writhing and shouting out in agony. His cries burned my ears, but I resisted the undeniable urge to plug my ears with my fingers. He didn't deserve to be blocked out, that would be disrespectful, making his humiliating death even worse and rewarding me with a guilty conscience.

Nearly half an hour, I predicted, later, every single one of the men was dead. Some had been outright kills, shots to the heart, head, neck, somewhere that would kill them instantly. Others had been drawn out, enduring several shots to either the leg, arm, foot, even the stomach, before draining the life out of them, agonisingly slowly.

When he had finished, I caught the look of sadistic pleasure that took over his face as his eyes scanned the crowd once more. He stopped momentarily on one person, letting his face contort with a sordid quality, his eye twitching in what could almost be mistaken as a wink. I felt immediately sorry for whoever that gesture had been aimed at.

"Well, I think that you've all grasped the message I was trying to put across." He laughed at himself, glancing behind him at the mutilated bodies and grinning.

"But," he let out a random gunshot, "let that be your final warning."

A scarily close choked gasp made my head whirl around as I witnessed a girl two people down from me fall forwards, dead. Jakob's head snapped just as quickly as mine had done, but his was filled with panic as he caught my eyes, instead of even casting a glance towards the dead girl.

In his expression, I could see the anxiety he was feeling. For a moment, he'd thought I could have been the one shot, and that's what had made him so apprehensive. Our eyes connected and I instantly spotted the relief as he breathed out a long sigh.

Then, he seemed to remember where we were and instantly returned his head forwards, breaking our gaze in case someone picked up on our silent communication.

I could still see the anger in the background of his emotions when he'd turned around though and so now I tried to figure out what was wrong with him.

My instant thought was that he was angry at being woken up. Childish, yes, and completely unrealistic also, but when I was going through the many possibilities, I decided it might be a contributing factor.

My next guess, was that it had something to do with making us witness this. As far as I was aware, Jakob was as much against everything that happened here as I was, he wouldn't necessarily want us to see such merciless killing. That was a much more realistic estimation and I knew that it was more than likely why he appeared so irate.

Another thought that came to mind, wasn't so positive, however. Maybe he was annoyed at these men for trying to revolt, to break free. Was he angry at them for trying to free themselves from such an atrocious place? I could assume that the inmates had known their fate before they even tried to rise up against the officers, but could Jakob be annoyed with them for trying? If that was the answer, then it lowered my opinion of him significantly.

Sighing, I waited for something else to happen. I was expecting more death, or at least some more firing of that infernal gun, which he'd already had to swap several times from using up all the ammunition in it.

But, nothing did happen. We were simply dismissed, led back to our huts by the same official who had taken us.

Since I had been at the back when we were coming, I was now at the front on the way back. Looking around at the many other girls who were now being returned to their respective huts, I caught sight of the horrified looks on most of their faces. All white as a sheet, they were positively terrified by what had just happened and using it to scare people away from following the dead men in their footsteps had definitely been a success.

Being one of the first to the reach our destination also meant that we were one of the last groups to return to our accommodation. When we got there, Jakob held the door open for us, so that he was ridiculously close when I passed through it.

He had his reasons though, which I soon found out when I heard his whisper close to my ear. "Come outside when everyone's asleep." He instructed, but not authoritatively, more like a request.

I replied with a subtle a nod, before entering the room and returning to my bunk.

It took a lot of effort not to fall asleep, because having already been awake talking to Jakob earlier, then woken once more to observe the horrible display, I was going to be even more exhausted than I normally was when it came to working time.

Still, I managed it, just because I was anxious to talk to Jakob. I wanted to know what he'd kept me, and him, awake for.

Although I often complained about being forced to work such long hours and endure the hardship that came with it, when I was awake, generally Jakob was too. He must work similar hours to the ones we did, as well as his late night rendezvous' with me. So, he should be just as exhausted.

The only difference was that he would have suitable rations to be working such long days on. He wouldn't be struggling to survive on meagre amounts of mouldy bread, the occasional lump of cheese and tiny portions of water. If his toned and muscly physique was anything to go by, then Jakob had more than enough food to eat.

Tip-toeing towards the door, I opened it a crack and slipped out. Jakob was sat on the stairs, in his now normal position, his face buried in his hands, which were propped up by his elbows on his knees.

He was so deep in thought that he didn't even hear the door creak momentarily. That was relieving because it meant that no one inside the shack was likely to hear it either.

Taking my customary seat beside him, he finally jolted out of his thoughts, offering me a small smile that still did wonders to make me feel better. "Guten abend." He offered, what I could only assume to be a greeting, in his native tongue.

"Jó éjszakát." I replied in Hungarian, using the language that if felt like forever since I had spoken. I found that my accent was more pronounced than I had expected and I liked the way the words felt on my tongue. Being so long since I'd spoken my first language, I'd forgotten how natural it was to me.

Jakob's lips quirked and he supplied me with a much bigger smile this time. "You should speak Hungarian more often." He repeated my original sentiments. "It sounds nice."

"Köszönöm," I couldn't help the grin that spread across my face as I thanked him. Then, my expression turned serious again as I recalled the nights events so far. "What's up?" I inquired, deciding I just needed to delve in an ask questions, the most original way of getting answers.

He shook his head, symbolising that he hadn't quite found the words yet. Instead of speaking, he just placed his head back in his hands and closed his eyes, a look of confusion contorting his expression. I noticed that the anger was gone, though, which was something I couldn't help but feel pleased about.

When my hand twitched, I realised what the unmistakable urge that I was feeling was. It was the urge to comfort him. My hand, off its own back, wanted to reach out and off some kind of support, whether that was to simply rub his back soothingly, or to remove his hat and run my fingers through his styled hair.

I held myself back, though, because I doubted such actions would provoke any kind of response from Jakob, but were more likely to distract him more.

After a couple of minutes, he finally lifted his head back up again, choosing to look me directly in the eyes. After a moments hesitation, he reached out and grabbed my hands in his own, averting his eyes to look down at those instead.

The warmth that spread through me, from only that minimal amount of contact, was overwhelming and I felt my mouth go dry, trying not to let my breathing become irregular. His hands were warm and callous as they massaged my own, a sign I interpreted as his own nervousness.

"Viktória," he began, his voice taught with some kind of emotion.

The way he appeared so nervous, made me anxious in turn. What was taking so much effort for him to say? Either way, it was worrying me.

"Viktória," he repeated, lifting his eyes now to gaze into my own. "When that shot went of earlier, I really thought that he'd shot you." The flash of despair in his eyes made my chest constrict tightly. He'd really been that afraid of me being shot? Surely he witnessed people dying everyday. What made me so special?

Then again, what made him so special compared to the other officers? I could be asking myself the same question.

"In that small moment, thinking that you were dead for a small instant, made me realise that I cared for you a lot more than I'd been admitting to myself."

I felt my breathing hitch and my heart rate increase scarily quickly. I resisted letting my jaw drop like I'd wanted to and resulted to just staring at Jakob wide-eyed, unsure of how to process such a confession. Inside, I was jumping for joy, disbelieving that Jakob could possibly have any sort of feelings towards me, but I couldn't quite bring myself to translate that to my exterior, yet.

After my lack of response, Jakob averted his eyes once more. "Of course I understand if you don't care about me. I'm working in this place, causing so much pain to so many people, I think I'd hate me in your position too."

He was beginning to ramble, which finally brought me out of my astounded stupor. Removing my hands from his own, and causing his face to drop even more with the assumption that I was repulsed by his touch, I moved them upwards and caressed the side of his face gently, a smile touching my lips.

Raising his eyes back to mine, I could see him resisting the urge to quirk an eyebrow. "I do care about you Jakob." I assured him, trying to convey the sincerity through my eyes.

The way his face lit up proved that I had succeeded and the genuine happiness that emanated from him made my heart leap. All the time that I'd spent with him, I'd never seen him look so honestly joyful. He'd showed signs of amusement, but never looked this delighted.

"Really?" He checked, trying not to let his smile slip when considering the prospect of a negative answer.

I laughed. "Really." I assured him.

The grin that spread across his face made him look even more unbelievably handsome than normal as he gazed unwaveringly into my eyes.

His hands, which were still resting in his lap from where I had let go of them, raised and he grasped hold of my waist gently.

Hesitantly, he brought me closer to him, so that we were mere centimetres apart. My hands, which were still holding his cheeks lightly, fell away so that I could wrap them around his neck instead, knowing already what his plan was.

Leaning forwards, he placed a tentative kiss on my lips.

Instantly, my cheeks flushed to an unnatural shade of red, but it wasn't from embarrassment, it was from the feelings that his kiss had elicited inside me. Whilst it was only a small kiss, which he pulled back from quickly, it still made my mouth water, my senses go mad for him.

Never, had I been given such a kiss and I was amazed something so simple could be so effective.

I noticed him checking my face then, checking if he'd done something wrong. Reassuringly, I pulled his mouth back to mine for a slightly longer kiss, one that had left me breathless by the end of it.

This time, we pulled back together and rested our foreheads against each others'.

"We shouldn't have done that." Jakob whispered, making my heart sink immediately. "But I don't regret it."

Chuckling, I had to find myself agreeing.

Even in the precarious situation we rested in, something as raw as that could never be apologised for.

Ah! I'd like to thank Modestieispurete for the idea for this chapter, it was great, so thankyou! I hope I didn't make it too morbid again though :(

But, good news, A KISS! They kissed! Amazing! I absolutely loved writing this chapter, so I hope you enjoyed reading it! Please Vote and Comment! See if I can get myself on the What's Hot list again!

Hope you enjoy this!

Chapter Ten

QUICK WARNING: This chapter contains rape. It doesn't go into much detail, but it's outlines what happens. So, when it gets to the italics skip past it if you don't want to read the details. I don't want to upset anyone. Thanks! :)

Chapter Ten...

Not being able to get last nights unexpected, yet completely enjoyable, kiss out of my head had not benefited my work rate whatsoever. I was now sporting more gashes on my hands from my lack of concentration than ever before, and I had managed to rip open already healing cuts as well.

So, although when it had happened it had been more than amazing, it didn't help me during work hours.

The fact I was nearly dropping off to sleep wasn't helping either. Having been awake talking to him, then being woken up again to witness the horrifying events of the rebellion, then talking, plus more, with Jakob again and then not being able to sleep because of the gazillion thoughts running through my head, meant that I was dead on my feet.

I wouldn't be surprised if I was the one who was collapsing and then being shot today.

I'd picked Jakob out as soon as I arrived this morning, positioned against the wall where he could stare directly at me; something he had definitely taken advantage of. I'd felt his eyes scanning my body for the majority of the time I'd been dismantling the many pairs of glasses that I dealt with in a day.

He'd sent me a few small smiles, which I'd just about managed to return without being noticed. When it came to getting our water, I was more than relieved to see that it was Jakob who was handing it out. He was no doubt subject to doing this because of his background. I could imagine that the other soldiers didn't think too highly of him.

It worked out well for me, however, as I was discreetly given a much bigger portion of water, which I made sure to gulp down quickly, for fear of being discovered and the trouble that I now realised it would bring Jakob's conscience.

I couldn't stop the blush that rose instantly to my cheeks as his fingers intentionally brushed mine when the water changed hands, causing me to curse myself mentally. Surely a blush was a sign of affection and I didn't want to be seen as giving Jakob any signs that might be considered caring.

"Thank you." I muttered, making sure he heard it, but no one else.

I received a small smile from him, but that was all, before I returned to my work station and carried on dismantling the spectacles and hoping that I didn't end up with no hands left by the time I'd finished.

*** *** *** *** *** *** *** *** *** *** *** *** ***

When I got back to my hut, I let myself go straight to my bunk and lie down, hoping to sleep for the whole night, probably for the first time since I'd been here.

Only, when I was drifting off nicely, my eyes nearly unfocused with exhaustion, my voice was spoken close to me. "Viktória!" Stephánia spoke, reaching out and shaking my shoulders gently. "Wake up!"

I groaned, annoyed that she had woken up what I thought might be my first night of proper sleep. "What is it?" I demanded, my voice harsher than I had meant, but carrying only a hint of the bitterness that was swirling around inside me.

Cracking my eyes open to look at Stephánia, I noticed the hurt in her eyes as she shook her head. "It's nothing, I'll go back to my own hut, I didn't want to disturb you." She muttered, prepared to climb back down the ladder and leave me alone.

I wasn't sure whether she was intending to guilt trip me, but it had worked and I held a hand out. "No, wait." I objected, forcing myself to sit up in the bunk bed. "I'm awake, just let me get up, we can sit on the bunk below." I suggested, gesturing to the bed below me.

When her face had disappeared from my view, I let the scowl sink back onto it. I did feel bad for being so cold towards Stephánia, but when she saw that I was asleep, wouldn't the more appropriate action have been leaving me alone because she could see that I was clearly exhausted?

Then another problem that I had, was that I couldn't exactly justify why I'd been so tired. As far as she was concerned, I'd had exactly the same amount of sleep as she had, so I had no reason to be so fatigued. She wasn't aware of mine and Jakob's late night get together, which had left me with even left of an incentive sleep.

Rearranging my face so that it was set in a pleasant smile, I followed Stephánia and sat on the bunk below. The bunk below mine was normally empty, because the girl who slept in it was always out of the hut, presumably talking to a friend like Stephánia talked to me. She was lucky to have someone that she could talk to like Stephánia and I were.

I knew that if it wasn't for Stephánia, and Jakob, I would be in a state right now. And how the people who currently had no one did it, I had no idea. I would have lost it by now if it wasn't for them both.

Joining Stephánia on the bunk, I fixed her with an expectant look. If she had woken me up, it had better at least be for a reason. "So, what's up?" I inquired, when she still didn't say anything.

Stephánia shrugged. "Nothing really." She admitted. "I only came to talk to you in general, I was bored."

Forcing myself not to glare flat out at her, I made myself chuckle. "Right." I agreed. "So…"

Stephánia averted her eyes and I saw the conflicted emotions in her eyes, before she just smiled in the same polite fashion that I had been. "I can't believe what happened with the mutiny last night." She stated, casting her mind back to the nights events.

Only, I found that when I tried to do the same, all I wanted to think about was Jakob. How he'd been so genuine, how his lips had moved against my own.

I'd always promised Adrian that I'd never open to my heart to anyone unless I felt more towards them than I did him, but it was safe to say that I felt just as much for Jakob as I did for Adrian. He was the main figure in my life now, and had been amazingly kind to me.

Stephánia carried on speaking, though, bringing me out of my fantasies of last night's kiss with Jakob. "That girl who they shot, she was practically next to you." A shudder rippled through both of our bodies at the possibility of my body being the lifeless one currently lying on the floor. "I don't what I'd be doing now without you." She admitted, shaking her head with horror. "I'd probably have begged to be shot down with you."

My eyes widened. "No, you wouldn't." I assured her. "You'd at least fight to carry on living, my death shouldn't ever affect that."

Stephánia looked at me, considering what I'd said. "I don't know if I could."

Telling her this, was almost hypocritical, since I'd only just been thinking how I wouldn't cope without her. The difference was, that I'd at least try. I would try and be okay, to keep living for as long as I could.

"You'd have to try." I told her sincerely. "You couldn't just give up like that."

Stephánia shook her head, her eyes still cast down at her lap rather than looking at me. "You're the only good thing in this place Viktória."

It was then that I realised how lucky I actually was. Not only was I privileged enough to have an old friend with me who could help me with things, but I also had Jakob. He was my source of information which I sometimes didn't want to know, he kept me marginally healthier than everything else without inflicting the same pain and abuse that everyone else had to deal with to get such treatment.

"I'm not going anywhere as long as I can help it." I told her, forcing out a smile. It wasn't forced because I was still annoyed at her for waking me up, but because I didn't want to think about whether Stephánia would lose her life or not. If I was getting extra rations and she wasn't, then surely she would be the one to go first.

A flash of guilt weighed in Stephánia's eyes then when she looked at me. "But," she began. "You're already skinnier than me. You're losing more weight than me. What if..." She trailed off and I knew that she couldn't bring herself to say what she was thinking.

Her statement made my eyes appraise her body. She was right. She did still have more meat on her than I did. What Jakob had said instantly came back to me. 'She's looking pretty well off considering how long you've been going without food already'.

My eyes narrowed and I set them on Stephánia. "Is there something you're not telling me?" I queried, eyebrow raised in expectation.

Immediately, she was shaking her head in denial. "No, why would you think that?"

"Because it is slightly weird how I'm so much skinnier than you." I pointed out.

"Why?" Stephánia queried, trying to look as confused as possible. "You're not that much thinner and it might just be that I was fatter when I first came in."

I muttered a curse word under my breath in Hungarian. All her excuses her valid. Without sharing the knowledge that I was also being sneaked extra stuff, I had no argument.

Stephánia regarded me curiously. "Are you hiding anything, Viktória?" She turned my question back onto me.

Doing exactly the same as she had, I shook my head in denial. "No, I just thought it was weird that's all. I mean I'm hardly malnourished compared to some of the people in here." I gestured subtly around the room.

He eyes followed mine as she took in the other inmates here. There bones were poking out all over the place and I could only imagine how visible their ribs were beneath the sacks we were clad in. You could see mine, but they weren't so stuck out that it was disgusting to look at. I still had a little bit of meat left on me.

I saw the shudder that visibly passed down Stephánia's spine and I knew that she could see the difference between us and them. Like Jakob had said, it quickly became obvious when people were getting special treatment. I had a feeling that was why Jakob wasn't feeding me ridiculous amounts and just enough to keep me healthy, but not make it quite so recognisable.

"You're right. But how are you so much better off than they are?" Stephánia asked, trying to redirect the questions away from her and towards me instead.

I shrugged. "I don't know. Maybe I've just been lucky." I lied, trying not to look incredibly guilty. "But what about you? You're even less thin than me. That has to mean something's going on."

Stephánia looked obstinate towards the idea of sharing what was really happening with me, but I had enough information to work it out. Jakob had been right in his predictions. Stephánia was being raped, she had to be. That was the only thing that made sense.

"Please tell me they're not." I muttered to myself, hoping that I was somehow incredibly mistaken.

If I was ever going to ask God for something, it would be that Stephánia wasn't being subject to such terror. I'd never been a religious person as most people from the village were. I'd always thought that the idea of there being something else out there was a ridiculous one. But, if there was something else that could stop this torture, then I would pray for it, and Stephánia's abuse, to stop.

Stephánia looked at me cautiously, but still refused to spill. "It must be coincidence." Was her only explanation. I knew that wasn't the truth though. My lack of under nourishment was no coincidence and neither was Stephánia's. There was something else going on there.

"Liar."

Tears pricked her eyes as she shook her head. "I'm not!" She denied fervently.

"Yes, you are." I had to get it out of her, to make sure that I was right, so I didn't torment myself wondering if my speculations were correct or not. More than that, I needed to comfort her. There had to be something that I could do to help.

"How would you know?" She suddenly pressed, raising an inquisitive eyebrow at me. "How would you know unless the same was happening to you?"

My eyes widened at her indirect confession. It was true. I was right after all. "Oh God, Stephánia, you're really being raped?"

Stephánia's eyes began to water, but she couldn't bring herself to give any other form of an affirmative answer. Instantly, I pulled her into a tight hug. That was when she let rip. The sobs rumbled through her body as tears poured from her eyes.

I found my own eyes following suit. This was the first time I'd seen anyone cry so openly since I'd arrived; everyone had been holding in their emotion and trying to stay strong. Now, though, I couldn't stop the despair seeping through.

I clung to Stephánia just as much as she was clinging to me and tried to stop my stupid blubbering. The door to the hut opened then, however, and Jakob appeared in the doorway, no doubt telling us it was time to get back to our huts.

When he instinctively looked over to my bed, however, and noticed the tears pouring from my eyes, he hastily invented an excuse, saying that he was inspecting bunks.

Scanning quickly through everyone else's and quickly reaching mine, he leant over, pretending to be looking at something more closely so that he could talk to me. "Are you okay?" He checked, ignoring Stephánia's presence completely.

When she heard the voice so close to her, she pulled back, and wiped her eyes, glancing unsurely at the person who had asked me the question. When she noticed it was actually Jakob, an SS officer who she thought had slapped me, her eyes narrowed. She didn't speak though and let me.

"I'm fine, honestly." I assured him.

Jakob glanced at Stephánia. "She has to go back to her hut." He stated regretfully.

Sighing, I knew he was right. But, I wasn't finished talking to her yet! I wanted to get more details, find out what was really happening. "Just one night." I begged. "I need to talk to her."

Remorse clouded his vision, but he still gave a swift shake of the head. "I'm sorry, Viktória, but I can't let her stay."

"She can sleep in my bed, no one will know." I pleaded, trying to appeal with my eyes. "Please Jakob."

He copied my sigh, but allowed me a small nod and slight smile. "If you get caught, you know what will happen, and it won't be pleasant." He warned, pain contorting his face slightly.

"As long as you're not getting blamed for it, I don't care."

"Come outside later, I need to talk to you." He told me, before leaning backwards and pretending to have finished what could only have been a very thorough search of the bed.

I nodded at him, offered a small and grateful smile, before he disappeared back out the door again.

"What was that about?" Stephánia inquired, suddenly reminding me that she was still present.

My cheeks flushed as I realised what we'd been saying while she was sat there. It was far too friendly for what she should have been witnessing. The fact we knew each other's names was surely inappropriate considering the situation.

"We're friends." I acknowledged her question.

She looked at me suspiciously. "He slapped you." She reminded me, as if I was crazy. "I meant what I said earlier, how would you know unless it was happening to you. Is that officer raping you?"

I shook my head vehemently. I knew Jakob would never do that. "No." I told her sincerely. "Definitely not."

Stephánia didn't look convinced as she regarded me dubiously. "But he slapped you, that's hardly the basis for a good friendship." She pointed out. "As well as the fact he's working in the place that's keeping us separated from our families," I felt my face twist guiltily as she said that, "making us work ourselves to exhaustion and randomly shooting people!" Her voice was quiet, but I could here how riled she had become.

I averted my eyes. When she put it like that, I knew she had a perfectly valid point. Why was I even friends with him, if not more. Then, I remembered all the good he had done for me, how much risk he had put upon himself to help me out. "He never slapped me."

"But I saw him!"

I shook my head. "No, you didn't." I contradicted. "He slapped his own hand, not my face."

Stephánia cast her mind back to the day and then nodded. "That makes sense. That's why you were holding your face so much, right? To hide that there was no mark."

"Precisely." I agreed.

"But, how would you even become friends with someone like that, knowing who he is and what he's done? He's a monster for working here." She accused, making me clench my fists.

Jakob wasn't a monster, Stephánia was just judging. Not that I could really blame her, from her obviously awful experiences. Thing is, I didn't like her talking about him like that. It wasn't something I liked to hear, especially when I knew how wrong she was. "It was work here, or be tortured and die." I stated bitterly. "Can you honestly say you would have chosen the latter?"

Stephánia looked at me warily, but eventually, she nodded in agreement. "Fair enough, I'm not going to bother asking for the story, but I can see why he did what he did." She conceded. "That still doesn't explain how you became friends in the first place, though."

I shrugged. "I was sat outside one night, when I couldn't sleep, and he came and talked to me. That's all." I explained, nonchalantly. It wasn't a big deal, but I could see why Stephánia was making it out to be.

She still looked to be shocked that I had managed to make a friend of one of the evil soldiers here, but I knew it wasn't like that. "So, you became friends after one meeting?" Stephánia clarified, not looking convinced.

I chuckled. "Of course not, it's happened a few times now."

"And that's how you're staying not thin, because he's feeding you more." She figured out, nodding as the wheels in her head spun.

I nodded. "Exactly. And that's how I knew about you, because he told me what he'd have to claim he was doing if people found out that he was giving me extra rations. I worked out that it must be what was happening to you." I returned our conversation to its original topic, determined to find out what was really going on with Stephánia. "Tell me what happened." I demanded, my voice soft, but stern.

Stephánia lowered her gaze again when it came back to the topic of her sexual abuse. "It was the second day we were here." She began, making me choke back a comment. I wasn't going to interrupt her, but second day? It had been going on that long without her telling me. "That man who slapped me in the morning, he came to me that night."

A shiver rippled up her spine as she cast her mind back to the events.

Stephánia sat outside her hut, arms wrapped around her knees, which we pulled up to her chin. In her first day, she'd already been subject to the monstrosities that were this place and it wasn't doing much to help her maintain the positive attitude she was trying to project onto Viktória, who was obviously suffering already. The light that had been extinguished in her eyes proved as much.

Whilst she wallowed, thinking of her family, the slap she'd received off that monster this morning, she failed to notice the figure approaching her. Too lost in her own thoughts that she didn't recognise the danger.

When she did, it was too late.

"Daring to break the rules again, are we?" A voice spoke from the shadows.

Stephánia's head swivelled on her shoulders as she sort out the source of the voice. When she did spot the stout figure leaning against the side of her hut, her hand instantly went to her cheek which was donning a bruise from the slap she had received this morning. She was too afraid to speak, so simply sat, horrified, instead.

When the soldier noticed her clutching her cheek, he let out a snort of grim laughter, remembering how he had been the one to inflict the injury on her that same morning. "Still hurt?" He inquired sarcastically, still staying propped up against the side of the rickety shack.

Stephánia still didn't respond with any sort of verbal comment, but the hatred in her glare was enough to convey what she would be saying otherwise.

"Yes, I thought it might." The officer mused aloud, his lips twisted with what could barely be associated with a smile. "But, I know something that will make you feel better."

The alarm bells were instantly ringing in Stephánia's head, but still there was nothing she could do to stop the events that would proceed. She was powerless, a feeling that no one likes. "I'm fine." She replied bitterly, knowing that it would do nothing, but having to try.

"No, no." The man insisted. "In fact, you don't have a choice, do you really?" He taunted, sneering maliciously at her. That was when he made his move, walking towards her at a slow pace - probably due to the stomach that was protruding over the waistline of his trousers.

Stephánia followed her natural instinct, which was to jump up and move backwards, to avoid him at all costs. That didn't go particularly well for her, however, as the man suddenly became much more agile, reaching out and grasping her arm with a vice like grip.

"I don't think so…" He trailed off, a sing-song quality to his voice as he played with her.

"What do you want with me?" Stephánia demanded, hating the fear and desperation that leaked out with her speech.

"I'm sure you'll find out in time." He offered her no explanation, furthering the apprehension that had built up inside her.

So, like any other person when they feel they're in danger, she opened her mouth, fully prepared to let out a full blown scream. Only, before a single sound could be heard, a hand had been slapped over her mouth, cutting off any noise that wanted to exit it. "Don't even think about it." He hissed, his voice showing how close his head was to her now.

She shivered, a gesture made not out of pleasure, but of pure disgust.

Then, she was being dragged, hauled by the bellicose general to god-knows-where. Despite all her struggling, she couldn't break free of his strong hold. She was never particularly strong and stood no chance against this man's clutch.

Not being able to speak, it was her mind which went through the endless possibilities, none being positive. As they passed by Viktória's hut, she wished that her friend would for some reason come out, do something that would protect Stephánia. That was no such thing that happened though and the man continued to tow her away, to an unknown location.

When they did reach their final destination, it turned out to be the official's bedroom, if it could be called that. Whilst it was an improvement on the cramped living conditions that Stephánia was currently dwelling in, it was hardly luxury. Complete with a small collection of candles which lit the room, a small bed and desk, there was barely enough room to move about in the room.

That didn't stop Stephánia trying, however.

As soon as the soldier had dragged the two of them into the room, locking the door behind him with a pair of keys that we're placed instantly inside his jacket, he released her. That was when she screamed, banging against the solid door hopelessly and kicking with all her might.

Sardonic laughter could be heard behind her as she didn't slack in her futile attempts to get free. She was not going to stay in here like a hopeless little girl who didn't fight back. She had to at least try, even if it was hopeless.

Stephánia could hear the laughter getting closer to her as suddenly a body was pressed up against her back. "There's no point in trying." The man told her casually. "You can't get out of this."

Stephánia still didn't hold back, though, her fists pounded unceasingly on the door, hoping that somebody, anybody would hear her. No one did, though, and no one saved her.

Suddenly, her whole body was flat against the door, so that her arms were forced up above her head. The officer's hands grabbed at her waist, and Stephánia screamed again, realising what was about to happen; the real reason she'd been dragged here.

"You have a very nice figure." The officer's mouth was at her ear, his stubble tickling her neck in a way that made her want to heave. His hands moved upwards, grasping hold of her breasts tightly and digging his nails in.

Stephánia let rip with another scream, even more petrified than she had been before.

"People can hear your screams." He told her. "But no one cares."

With that, he released his arms from her, which she instantly took advantage of, bashing against the door once again.

Only, whilst she was doing that, she failed to notice how the officer was now undoing his pants, letting them drop to the floor and revealing his arousal. He moved back towards Stephánia and pushed against her once more, letting her feel the hardness against her back.

Panic and horror filled her mind as her breathing became to come out fast with dread. This couldn't be happening. Not to her. Her first time was supposed to be with someone that she loved, someone she cared deeply about, someone she wanted to give her virtue to. Not some forty old man who was forcing her into something, with the full intent of hurting her.

Yelps of terror emanated from her mouth, but like he'd said, no one cared. In fact, people were probably revelling in her screams of dismay in nearby rooms.

He hoisted up her flimsy dress, becoming fed up of her screams and wanting to get some physical, rather than just mental, enjoyment out of her.

She knew what was coming and squeezed her legs together with such a force she didn't think possible. It did little to deter him though and she cringed as she felt his hand running up her thigh to its intended destination.

Only, it never got there, because Stephánia made one final effort at getting him off her. Raising a leg which wasn't trapped my his body, she sent it right into her own intended destination, kicking him right in the place she knew it would hurt the most.

Much to the contrary of her hopes, it did little to deter him. Shouting in agony, the general peeled Stephánia's body from the door and tossed her onto the bed with little effort. All she'd succeeded in doing was riling him up, making him angry, so that now he wasn't in the mood for teasing her. He was just ready to take her, and all her innocence.

Lying now on her back, Stephánia didn't have the opportunity to lift herself up, before the soldier had put his whole body weight back on her. She clamped her legs shut, but the general didn't care for that, forcing them open with no effort now he was done with the taunting.

He pinned them there, looking down at her body. Her dress had come up to reveal her breasts in the kafuffle as well, so now he was even more aroused than before.

Leering shamelessly at her, he pointed his tip at her opening. Although he was going to play with her a bit first, let her at least become aroused to a point, he wanted to see her writhe in pain now. See her screams of agony. It would be like an aphrodisiac and he knew it.

Giving her one last sadistic smirk, he gave a thrust, forcing the whole of his length inside her without room for hesitation. He could feel her rip as he went, but it proved to stimulate him more, as a loud groan tore from his mouth.

It was nothing compared to her scream of absolute agony, however, and her shrieks continued to overpower his cries of ecstasy throughout the whole thing.

I listened in horror as Stephánia recapped her first encounter with the abusive bastard. She was once again sobbing by the end of it and I tried to calm her down to no avail. It was now that I wished I hadn't persuaded her to tell me. Making her relive that was something I wouldn't wish on anyone, especially Stephánia.

I thought back to last nights events and realised that it was Stephánia the general at the front had been winking at and shivered with disgust. All that time, it was that slap, which Stephánia had only endured because she was walking to me, that started it off. He would've targeted someone else if it wasn't the for the slap. He might have targeted me instead, which I would have preferred. Better me than her.

"I'm so sorry Stephánia." I whispered, my voice choked with both guilt and sorrow. I couldn't even imagine such events, but Stephánia's recount had been enough to prove how terrible the ordeal had been.

"He's done it again, three times now." She informed me, her whole body shaking with the memories. "And he'll do it again. Many times."

"If I could do anything, then I would." I assured her. "If I could take your place, then I would."

Stephánia shook her head wildly. "There'd be no point in that. I'm scarred now, no point in doing it to us both."

Whereas I could fault her logic, I didn't see the point. She would just continue to argue with me and it would be to no avail. Besides, I couldn't say that I was as willing as I made out to take her place. Despite saying and thinking that I would do it if I had the chance, I wasn't sure if it came to the reality if I would be so generous. It was hardly something to go into willingly.

"Look, Stephánia, you should go to sleep." I suggested, taking in her incredibly weary figure. All the explaining, the memories, they'd taken their toll on her, that was for certain. And whilst I was probably just as tired, I still had one last thing to do before I could go to sleep.

Stephánia nodded in agreement. "I am exhausted." She admitted, her eyelids already beginning to drop.

"Mine's the top bunk." I told her, gesturing to the bed above where we were sitting. It was only now that I put any thought into where the girl who should be occupying where we were currently sitting was. She was hardly ever here, but I honestly didn't have the energy to think of her whereabouts right now.

"Okay, you said you'd share with me, so are you coming to bed now?" She inquired. Then, she answered her own question before I had time to. "Oh, right, you've got to meet that soldier." She remembered.

"His name's Jakob." I informed her.

"I know." She said. "But I can't bring myself to give them names. If all they want to remember us by is numbers, why should we be any different?"

"Because Jakob is different." Was my final response, before I got up and snuck outside, awaiting Jakob's arrival.

Hehe, whoops! Took a bit of a long time updating there, but it is an extra long chapter, so that kind of makes up for it? Hopefully? Anyway, about the rape thing. I know it's a bit morbid and stuff, and some of you would rather that I hadn't included it at all, but its something that would have happened, plus it helps to progress the story line, in a dark kind of way. There's just limited plotline ideas for such a story, so I'm taking them where I can.

For people who read the italics bit, I hope it wasn't to in depth? I wanted to get the emotion, but not necessarily go into too much detail. It is PG-13.

Aside from that, hope you enjoyed it! And please vote and comment! This story is becoming increasingly popular, it's great! I'm actually on the Watty Awards What's Hot list, an achievement if I do say so myself, considering there of nearly 30,000 entries!

I know I'm not going to win, but doing marginally well is acceptable as far as I'm concerned!

Hope you enjoy this chapter! Vote for length is what I say ;D

Chapter Eleven

C hapter Eleven...

Just as I'd expected, Jakob was sat on the stairs, staring straight ahead and resting his head on his hands. Even from the back I could tell that he was deep in thought, which made me hesitate to make my presence known.

It didn't take long for him to notice I was stood there, however, and he turned around, smiling warmly, but with a hint of concern, at me. "Guten abend Viktória." He greeted me, his eyes showing the worry his face refused to let slip.

"Jó estét, Jakob." I returned what I assumed was the same thing. I could guess good evening in most languages.

"Are you okay?" Jakob launched straight into what he was dying to know, the anxiety now becoming dominant on his face as he regarded me closely. "You were crying earlier and..." His expression contorted with further upset.

I couldn't help but smile at his obvious alarm and in that moment, I realised just being in his presence soothed me considerably. "I'm fine." I assured him genuinely. I was okay now. Still obviously devastated by the knowledge Stephánia was raped so heartlessly, but better in my own mind. "Stephánia, she just…" I trailed off, not even being able to finish the sentence.

Maybe I wasn't as okay as I thought.

Jakob sighed, already guessing what I'd put off saying. He wrapped a tentative arm around my shoulder and pulled my into his side comfortingly. "I was right, then." He stated, not sounding pleased about that fact.

I copied his exhalation of air and nodded. "Yeah." I agreed regretfully. "The man who shot that girl practically next to me last night." I shuddered at the memory and the realisation that suddenly dawned on me. "Stephánia must have been the girl he winked at, oh God."

I felt myself shrink into Jakob's side even further as the awareness grasped me. I'd missed all the small signs that could've led me to the conclusion faster. "It's okay." Jakob soothed, his voice but doing little for the guilt that weighed up inside me. "You couldn't help not knowing that."

I shook my head vehemently. "It's not okay." I argued, scowling at my own stupidity. "I should have been there for her, she's been going through so much and I never even knew. She's still so positive, how does she managed that? She doesn't deserve to have that done to her, I should be the one in her place." I ranted, on and on with the emotions that gripped me.

I had to get it out. I'd been bottling my emotions up for too long now, and here they were, back for vengeance. I was breathing heavily when Jakob interrupted me. "Wait, wait, stop." He instructed, cutting me off. "You do not deserve any harm brought to you."

I glanced up at his face and saw the pain that entered his expression, presumably at the thought of being harmed.

"If someone did that to you." He shook his head to show the lack of words he could find, but his face was so full of anger just at the thought of it I could barely comprehend the sudden change in emotion. "I'd have to murder them."

His body had become tense and rigid against me now and I knew that prospect wasn't one he could easily picture.

"No you wouldn't." I disagreed. When he opened his mouth to argue, I justified my statement. "If you murdered someone, you'd be killed yourself." I pointed out. "And if someone did that to you." I faced the same lack of words now, unable to put what I would feel into speech. "I couldn't deal with that." I decided on finally.

"Lets just hope it never comes to that." He stated eventually. "But if someone did…rape you." He faltered over the word. "You would tell me, wouldn't you?"

I hesitated. Would I tell him? With the knowledge of what he'd do, I honestly wasn't sure. Plus, I'd never want to put that kind of burden on him. Then again, the emotional support he would provide me with was enough to rival all those reasons. "I don't know." I answered honestly.

He gave me a flat look. "You'd have to tell me Viktória."

I shook my head. "No, I wouldn't." I contradicted. "I wouldn't want to make you feel that guilt. Don't you already feel bad enough for me being in this place?" I reminded him of the many times he'd expressed that remorse, if not directly.

He sighed. "Yes, but still, I'd want to help you Viktória."

"And I'd want you to help me too." I agreed. "But I wouldn't want to burden you either."

He just tightened his arm around me, which told me he wasn't going to continue arguing, to some extent, with me. "I did some digging into the twins thing." He informed me on a completely different subject, a grimacing now showing on his face, which didn't look good as far as I was concerned.

I hesitated before questioning his new found knowledge. "What did you discover?" I inquired, already dreading what he was about to say. From what I'd learnt about this place so far had all been negative and so I assumed this would follow the trend.

Jakob removed the hand from my shoulder so that he could rest his elbows on his knees and bury his head in his hands, removing the hat on his head and running his fingers through his hair. I took this as an extremely bad sign and reached out, boldly putting a hand on his leg, near to where his elbow was propping up his head.

"Just tell me." I told him, my voice was soft in what I wanted to be an encouraging tone. "It'll be better if you get it out there." I assured him with what I hoped was the truth.

He raised his head marginally and twisted it to the side, gazing at me unwaveringly. "Viktória, this is horrific." He stated unfalteringly. "This is worse than anything I've told you about this place so far. Worse than the killing, worse than the rape."

Now I was cautious. I hadn't expected anything much worse than that. What could be worse than that? Worse than the appalling events I'd been enlightened on. I couldn't thing of much. "I…" I started, still unsure of what to say. "Just tell me." I repeated my earlier phrase.

I should be being selfish enough to protect myself when I knew Jakob needed to let it out, let out the obvious anger he had towards these people.

After a long and drawn out sigh, hesitation and clear deliberation in his face, he lifted his head and turned towards me, so that my bare knees were touching his trouser clad ones. He grabbed a hold of my hands with his own, in what would become a support for the both of us.

"Okay." He agreed, preparing himself. "The last time I saw another officer long enough to talk to him, I queried him on it." He didn't elaborate on that, but I knew he would have been subtle about it. He didn't want to risk any more than he already was and I didn't want him to either. If anything happened to him, because he'd been doing something for me, I would be insanely guilty for as long as I lived.

"Go on." I prompted him gently when he stopped speaking.

"He gave me a rundown on what happened to twins when they're taken from the judenrampe. The soldiers that lead them away take them to the medics here."

I almost snorted at the idea. "Medics?" I queried. "I somehow doubted there'd be medics here."

Jakob let out a small and strained chuckle. "I guess medics isn't the right word. Doctors, or physicians maybe?" He struggled to find the right word in English. "An arzt."

I nodded, telling him that I understood and giving him the sign to continue.

"These arzts, they do experiments on the twins, to see how far their genetic connection reaches and to try and discover what happens to one if something happens to the other." He explained. I saw the physical shudder that passed up his spine, and I squeezed his hands tighter. I obviously hadn't heard the worst of it yet.

"What kind of experiments?" I dared to ask, hoping I wasn't pushing Jakob too far and that I wasn't about to scar myself for life as well.

Jakob shook his head. "Freezing people, dipping them in freezing tanks for hours on end. Giving people only sea water and seeing if they can survive. Removing nerves, mutilating and disabling people. And with the twins, sometimes sewing them together, trying to make conjoined twins."

I could understand why Jakob had been tentative in voicing the information now. That was worse than atrocious and he was right, it was worse than anything I'd been told about so far. All that was happening to those people was torture, pure torture, for the purpose of pointless medical experiments.

"Then the officer I asked, he took me to the rooms."

I felt my face twist, just as Jakob's did, when he revealed that. Surely not. Surely Jakob hadn't witnessed the horror himself. Seen all those people in those conditions, the sheer agony they must have gone through.

"Ó, Istenem." I muttered the 'oh god; in my native tongue, that shocked I couldn't utter anything else. "Please tell me you didn't see."

He was now clutching my hands so hard that some of the gashes I had from dismantling the thousands of spectacles were re-opening, but I didn't mind. If that was what he needed to do to keep slightly sane, then it was fine by me. "I saw them all." His mind was far away now and he wasn't talking to me, he was talking to himself. "The children, being forced into the freezing water and their screams." He shivered in revulsion and sympathy. "The experiments gone wrong were the worst. The people with eyes missing, limbs disfigured or gone completely. I even saw someone die."

I gazed at his face and could see the mental torture he was enduring. "You don't have to say it." I assured him, realising now that getting him to speak about this might not have been such a good idea. He was making himself suffer.

"No," he argued, his voice barely a whisper. "I have to do this." He convinced himself, staring directly into my eyes, but still being slightly unfocused.

"Okay."

"They were taking a nerve from a man's back. I watched as he writhed in pure agony, there was no anaesthetic. When they took it, I saw him go rigid up to the neck. They'd paralysed him and the blood was pouring from the wound they'd made. He was still screaming though. Screaming from the shock that he suddenly couldn't move. And I witnessed it, as his face lost all colour and he bled to death. I had the opportunity to turn away, but I couldn't. What kind of person does that make me Viktória?"

When I realised what he was getting at, I stared at him incredulously. "You're a normal person!" I exclaimed. "Anyone would stare, it's just one of those things, you hate watching it but you have to because of that. Don't you dare put any of the blame for this on yourself." I warned, narrowing my eyes as he prepared an argument.

"But I watched and I didn't do anything to stop it." His voice was broken and I knew he was trying not to let on how badly this had actually affected him.

"There was nothing you could have done." I reminded him. "Not unless you wanted to be the next person in that room being frozen to death."

"I probably should have been."

I sighed, but refused to give in. If he carried on with this mindset, he really would end up doing something he'd regret in the long run. "Stop it." I demanded. "Stop hating yourself for things you can't control. Hate them instead, hate them for being the ones doing it."

"Oh, I do." He assured me bitterly and with such conviction I definitely believed him. "But then there's the issue, who's worse? The person committing the crime, or the person who just stands by and lets it happen?"

"It doesn't matter in this situation, because if you stood up to them, what would come of it? You'd be killed, end of. They'd end you instantly for risk of bad consequences. How would that help those people? It wouldn't. You'd be dead and I'd be-" I stopped myself. What would I be? I'd be nothing, but I couldn't quite bring myself to admit that yet.

Jakob shook himself out of his trance-like state of guilt then and stared at my clearly distraught face. The way he was talking, he genuinely sounded as though he might do something stupid. If he did, he wouldn't be given another second chance.

He'd be gone.

Dead.

He released my hands and pulled me into a tight hug. "I'm sorry." He apologised, for what, I wasn't quite sure yet. Either way, it did comfort me considerably and I just hoped he wasn't about to say he was going to commit suicide by speaking his views.

I gripped him just as forcefully and revelled in the feel of his hands brushing against my exposed skin - which was a lot when you took into the account the rag we were expected to wear as our clothing.

"I shouldn't have unloaded all of that on you." He explained his earlier apology. "I won't doing anything silly." He assured me. "I wouldn't do that to you, plus I know I'm not brave enough. I'm far too much of a coward to actually do anything about any of this, the fact I'm working here is proof enough of that."

I sighed against his shoulder. "You are not a coward." I ensured him cogently. "If you're a coward for that, then the rest of the world is just as much."

"My dad didn't care. He went through all of that for a cause. Why should I have been any different?" He pointed out correctly.

He did have a point there, but I still didn't condemn him. I couldn't. "Your father was obviously a hero, but that still doesn't mean you're a coward." I tried to justify my own reasoning.

"Yes, I am." He continued to argue stubbornly.

"Well not to me." I finalised.

He pulled away and moved his hand to caress my cheek instead. Moving forward, he gave me a tender peck on the lips, that left me begging mentally for more. "I don't think you realise how much that means to me." He announced quietly, his voice as intimate as our meeting of lips had just been.

I allowed a small smile to grace my face as he gave me another quick kiss. Even though we hadn't discussed the possibility of any kind of relationship between us, these small romantic moments were good enough for me and I basked in them.

He grinned, his face lighting up with the first positive emotion I'd seen in him all night, genuine happiness. "I'm glad I met you Viktória."

"I'm glad I met you too Jakob." I agreed, smiling also with pure joy.

As horrible as this place was and the atrocities that came with it, these little snippets of sheer bliss were enough to keep my going through the next day.

We both leaned in, our lips meeting in the third kiss of the evening.

Only this one wasn't quite so perfect, because an almost inaudible gasp interrupted one of our cherished embraces, making us both freeze in terror.

I HAVE EVENTUALLY UPLOADED. Yes, it's not even a long chapter, I'm afraid, but it's better than nothing.

And I have a new cover, made by...moi! Tell me if you prefer this or the other one, because I'm generally rubbish at making covers!

So, this chapter reveals what's happening to Stephania's twins, and obviously lots of Jakob and Viktoria, YAY! Hope it was okay, and I'm sure you pretty much know who's caught them at the end!

Enjoy, vote and comment!

Thanks!

Chapter Twelve

C hapter Twelve...

Stephánia stood in the doorway, her face pale with shock and her eyes wide.

Jakob and I were instantly separated, eyes averted and not even daring a glance at the other's face. Thoughts were rushing through my head, much like they would be in Jakob and Stephánia's the same.

What was Stephánia thinking? I'd told her we were friends and she'd thought nothing more of it. Truth be told, I wasn't even sure what Jakob and I were at the moment, but just friends wasn't the category I'd put us under.

What was Jakob thinking? He was risking a lot by even talking to me, never mind having the emotions he'd briefly expressed towards me. Stephánia catching us would no doubt bring back the reality of how risky this was. Would he want to stop associating with me now?

What was I thinking?

Honestly, I was too caught up with everyone else's thoughts to be delving into my own complicated ones. The two people in front of me were now the most important in the world as far as I was concerned and their opinions were far more significant to me than my own.

Nothing was said for nearly five minutes, everyone too involved in their own minds, or trying to predict their companies thoughts like I was. Either way, the silence was beyond awkward and I began to shuffle with anxiety.

I tapped my fingers against the hard wood beneath me as a nervous habit, until another hand covered my own and Jakob gave me an exasperated look. "That is really annoying." He muttered, his German accent so heavy I could barely comprehend what he was saying.

I bit my lip, another edgy tendency I possessed. "Sorry," I replied, my accent also more pronounced, because I was so caught up with emotion that I wasn't concentrating on my English.

In that slight conversation, Jakob and I had shared a brief and silent communication via our eyes. He'd told he was worried, scared that Stephánia's knew found knowledge might be the end of us. I'd been reassuring, making sure he knew he wouldn't suffer because of this.

The only thing that would take the strain now, would be mine and Stephánia's friendship. Her trust in me would be rightfully dinted now and it would take some time for it build up again. She'd confided in me about her sexual abuse, and I'd kept quiet about something that wasn't half as bad. In fact, Jakob and I wasn't bad at all.

Our short exchange, Stephánia had snapped out of her stupor of alarm and come back to the reality of where she was. She glanced between Jakob and I, still speechless, then glared at me.

"You were kissing a German soldier, Viktória." He words were a statement, but her voice was accusing and bitter. "As if that's not bad enough, why didn't you tell me?"

I was speechless, stumped as to how I was supposed to explain this to her. She didn't understand, because she didn't feel what I felt and her head was tainted by her experiences.

Obviously I could comprehend her hatred of all the SS soldiers here. Had I been in her position, I would have been the same. But I knew things that she didn't and I was in a completely different mindset to her when it came to this.

All that I could manage to utter was a feeble apology. "I'm sorry." I whispered, pleading with her to understand with my eyes. I needed her to realise that I did have my reasons, that this was a genuine friendship, or more, not whatever she had decided mine and Jakob's relations were.

"That's not an explanation." Her voice wasn't loud enough to disturb anyone else or to attract attention, but its pitch had raised a notch and she was letting her anger show.

"I don't know what you expect me to say!" I retorted, trying not to sound too inconsiderate, but also telling the truth. "You just saw what we did, you know what happened, what else is there to say?"

"Why didn't you tell me?" She repeated her earlier question, eyes boring into mine intensely as she waited for something of explanation.

"I don't know!" I exclaimed, my voice having also risen in pitch but my volume not increasing. "I was scared, I didn't want to risk anyone else finding out. I don't even know what this is." I gestured between Jakob and I. "I wanted to be sure before I told you."

Stephánia's look softened momentarily, before her riled appearance came back for vengeance. "That's just an excuse." She stated, convincing herself as she spoke. "It looked pretty clear to me what this was, and so I can't understand why you didn't say anything! You're supposed to trust me. I told you everything, and you didn't even say a word about this."

I could see the tears beginning to glisten in her eyes and I knew she was right. She'd spilled her heart to me just this evening, coming clean about her sexual abuse, but I'd held back. Not because I didn't trust her exactly, but because I was unsure and nervous. I needed to find out the facts of mine and Jakob's relationship before I went repeating them to Stephánia.

"I didn't know what to tell you." I admitted. "And you were so upset. I didn't know how you'd take this, so I thought I should leave it a while."

Just as Stephánia opened her mouth to make another retort, Jakob cut her off. "You both need to go inside." He instructed, eyes locking with mine. "There'll be a patrol around here soon and if someone sees you out here, you know what the consequences range to."

He sent a pointed look at Stephánia then who understood perfectly. She'd been in this position the first time she'd been assaulted. "Okay." I agreed, trusting Jakob's word immediately.

Jakob stood up and I followed suit, forcing myself to my feet and glancing up at Jakob, who towered above me. He gave me a reassuring smile and his arm came out to rub my shoulder soothingly. "I would have stayed at talked but you know I have to go." His tone was apologetic and his eyes didn't wander from my own.

He pulled me into a quick hug, which I eagerly returned. His head, once again clad in his uniform's hat, rested on my hair and his lips came just above my ear. "Just tell her the truth." He advised me. "Tell her how you feel honestly and she'll understand."

I nodded against his chest. That would be the best idea. If I lied anymore, then I'd just be digging myself into an even bigger hole and Stephánia's trust in me would deplete even more.

Jakob pulled back and gave me another, quick, supportive smile and an even quicker peck on the lips. "Ich liebe dich." I barely heard him mutter before he had turned away and strode off down through the many rows of huts, after telling me he'd talk to me tomorrow.

That was a piece of German I hadn't learnt, but I didn't bother pondering it. It probably was just a statement of good luck.

Stephánia, who had been observing our exchange intently, glanced at me when Jakob was gone and gave me a particularly grim look. "Lets go inside." She suggested, her voice still cold as she gestured at the door.

I nodded solemnly and followed her in, reaching our bunk and realising the bottom one was still empty. Whoever was supposed to be sleeping there hadn't returned, for whatever reason I wasn't sure.

Deciding it would be safer to stay on the lower bed, rather than to traipse up the ladder and risk disturbing people, we settled down opposite each other. Normally I would have had my legs crossed, but the lack of underwear I had and the shortness of my dress prevented that.

"Tell me everything." Stephánia demanded as soon as we had lapsed into silence. Her voice had softened marginally as she looked at me expectantly. As mad as she probably still was, she'd at least had the sense to realise she should get the facts before making a judgement.

"Well, there's not much to say really." I told her honestly. The scarily little amount of time that we'd been here meant there hadn't been many opportunities for us to meet. The time we had spent together had mainly been talking about the monstrous events that took place here. Obviously, that was some knowledge I would be sparing Stephánia of though, so that gave me even littler to say.

"The first day we were here, being put into our lines, that was when I first saw Jakob, he was one of the officers behind the desk."

Stephánia nodded with remembrance. "Igen." She muttered her agreement. "He was there when I was being sorted as well. I still remember he didn't look as excited about the twins as the other one did. He seemed to be in the background the whole time."

"That's because he hates it here." I stated, before realising I hadn't quite gotten to that part of the story yet. "But anyway, then when we worked the first day, he was handing out the rations and he gave me more than everyone else." I still wasn't entirely sure why he'd done that, but I hadn't questioned it and I probably never would. I was just grateful that he'd singled me out. Anyone would be lucky to have that kind of support here, minus the event that normally came with it.

I carried on telling my tale, becoming more lost in the memories as I went on. "Then that same night, he came when I was sat outside." I'd already pretty much told Stephánia this bit when I'd explained our friendship, but this time I'd go into a little bit more detail. "He told me about why he was working here in the first place."

Stephánia gave me an expectant look. "Are you going to tell me why?" She inquired sarcastically.

I hesitated. Would Jakob want me to tell Stephánia? It seemed like a pretty personal tale, but if I wanted her to believe he was a good person really, then the explanation might work in my favour. "I don't know…" I trailed off, hoping she didn't get mad at me. I could already see the incredulity building in her eyes though and so I decided to recap it before she had time to speak.

"His father worked for Abwehr against Hitler and plotted an attempt on his life. He was caught out, tortured and killed. Jakob was given the option to either suffer the same fate or come and work here."

Unlike how I'd imagined that would soften her harsh view on him, her face became immediately aghast. "What a coward!" She exclaimed. I'd already told her part of this during the justification of our friendship, but that had been much briefer. Now she had the full tale she'd formed a completely different opinion. "How could he betray all that his father stood for so easily?"

"He hates himself for it." I told her honestly. He'd expressed his guilt many times and I'd seen the remorse that haunted his eyes constantly. It wasn't a decision he'd easily lived with.

"Well then why doesn't he take that gun to his head? That would solve his guilt pretty easily." She pointed out bitterly.

I sighed, but I'd come up with the same response mentally as well. But, he was afraid of death, which was an explanation in itself. In all honesty, he probably should be labelled a coward, but if anyone else was put in his shoes, they would no doubt do the exact same thing.

"Can you honestly say you'd be prepared to shoot yourself through the head? Just so you could stick to your dad's principals?"

She weighed it over, but then nodded. "Yes, yes I could. Anything would be better than working here."

I knew there was no point in arguing, because she wasn't about to budge from her opinion, so I might as well carry on the recapping of our meetings and see if I could make her form a better opinion of him.

"Anyway," I cut short our argument of morals. "After that meeting, we saw each other again a few times at night. We just talked about stuff. He faked slapping me."

That reminded her of something good he had done for me that she couldn't deny. "He risked a lot to do that." She stated thoughtfully.

"I know." I grimaced. I was obviously grateful that he hadn't, but if it came around again, I would want him to just slap me. It wasn't worth the risk when he could just inflict a small wound on me. "He really shouldn't have done that."

Stephánia shook her head wryly. "You're ridiculous. Why wouldn't you want him not to hurt you?"

"If he'd been caught, he would've been given something far worse than a slap. It would be better if he'd just got it over and done with and hit me."

"I suppose." Stephánia admitted doubtfully. "But I wouldn't be complaining about it."

I knew she was only saying that because she hadn't gathered the understanding Jakob and I shared yet, so she was still holding her hostile opinion of him. "We kept speaking at night time, until one day, he admitted that he cared about me." I couldn't help but smile automatically at the memory, trying not to feel guilty when I realised it was because we'd been talking about what had happened to Stephánia's sisters. "And I told him about Adrian."

Stephánia regarded me curiously, knowing how much of a soft spot the topic of Adrian was to me. "You told him about Adrian?" She reiterated dubiously.

I nodded. "Yeah." I admitted. I'd been wary about telling him, but when I had, it had lifted a weight off my shoulders. As much as Adrian's death had saddened me, I loved talking about him, especially to someone who knew nothing about him and hadn't heard my stories thousands of times before.

"I'm surprised."

I shrugged. "I like talking about Adrian." I reminded her.

"Not to just anyone you don't."

"Jakob's not just anyone." With that point, I moved the story on once more. "The night of the mutiny, Jakob thought I'd been the one to get shot." I winced at the memory of the girl falling down beside me, lifeless. "We talked that night and he kissed me."

I blushed as Stephánia narrowed her eyes at me. "I can't believe you've been kissing a German soldier Viktória."

"You can't only identify him as a German soldier." I complained. "He has a name and he had an identity. He's not just one of the crowd, haven't I just explained that?"

Stephánia shook her head. "How do you know he's not just using you? How do you know he's not just waiting to do exactly what that bastard did, does, to me?" She queried, raising an eyebrow at me. Her voice had become suddenly bitter and I knew this was why she was finding it hard to see Jakob as a human being worth anything more than the excrement polluting the disgusting toilets we were forced to use.

"Because Jakob's not like that. If he wanted to take advantage of me, he could have just done it the first time he saw me. He has that power and if he wanted to use it, then he could." I reminded her. "As it is, he's barely even put a gentle finger on me. I know he wouldn't hurt me."

That was something I was sure of and didn't even worry about. It was a definite fact Jakob had gone out of his way not to hurt me. He wouldn't suddenly go back on that.

Stephánia was still understandably cynical though. "I don't trust him."

"I do."

"Fair enough, but you can surely comprehend my scepticism?"

"I can." I admitted. "I know what you've been through now and I get that you don't people easily anymore, especially a German soldier. But, I know him better than you do and I trust him, with my life." I tagged the last bit on as a real emphasis of how much I meant this.

My life might not mean much to anyone anymore, but it was still a big statement, especially when it was truthful. When it came down to it, I did trust Jakob with my life.

And I dared to think that he would do the same.

Hehe, whoopsy again on the long update, but, the next few chapters will be the penultimate ones, which yes, means this story is nearly at the end now! I'm guessing it will get to around 20 chapters, but I have it all worked out in my head now, so I really want to start writing it down!

This chapter was insanely boring, but I'm kinda' hoping the next ones will make up for it!

Thanks for the votes and comments, I love them all! Please donate some more here ;D

Oh, and I put a little something in there that I'm wondering if anyone will have picked up on, awaiting your comments ;D

Chapter Thirteen

C hapter Thirteen...

I sat on the steps, waiting as I did nearly every night now for Jakob to arrive. It had been three days since Stephánia had found out about Jakob and I, and whatever we were, but she'd become increasingly tolerant, thankfully.

Whereas she couldn't quite bring herself to accept that I had feelings for a German soldier, she could at least ignore it as best she could, without making some comment expressing her doubt and uncertainty, which had been her first resort after I'd explained everything to her.

Avoiding talking about it was something I was happy to do anyway. It wasn't something I was comfortable speaking about, not when I was so unsure about it. There were so many risks involved, and I still wasn't sure exactly what it was Jakob and I were doing. It was obvious we couldn't be together, there'd be no point in that; we barely found time to speak as it was.

We were just friends, with some added bits. We were friends who'd kiss, who'd confess to having more than just friendly feelings towards one another.

Yes, that was exactly what we were.

I rested my head against my drawn up knees as I waited for Jakob to arrive. The last couple of nights, we'd just talked, and hugged, and kissed. It had been surprisingly peaceful, as we just spent the time learning more about each other. Because, although we'd got a good knowledge of each other's personality and characteristics, our pasts were unknown, never having the time to discuss them before. I only knew snippets of his and he only knew snippets of mine.

So, we spent time delving into our pasts, seeing the similarities and differences, despite the obvious variations.

Although Jakob's mum had not died giving birth to him, like mine, she'd died when he was at an early age and he couldn't even create an image of what she looked like in his head anymore. That meant his father was the only one who'd been around for him as well; and why the weight of his guilt bared so heavy on his conscience. He'd betrayed the only living relative he'd even known.

Aside from losing our mothers at an early age, there weren't really any other similarities between our lives before we met. Whereas I'd lived in the small town of Ajka, buried away in the mountains, excluded from all the goings on in the world, Jakob had been living in Berlin, the heart of the war effort. He knew all about the fighting, his father being involved in Abwehr, and he'd even been bombed by the English, a house next door to him destroyed beyond repair.

In Ajka, we'd not witnessed any bombing, the sirens in the distance being the only reminder to us that it was actually happening, and the fires that you could just see from on top of our hill. To think Jakob had almost lost his house, and quite possibly his life, from that was quite frightening.

If I hadn't had Jakob here, no doubt I would have been almost dead by now, like all the other people, bar Stephánia, were. The people in our hut's bones were sticking out now, protruding from the skin, and it was more than obvious that they were undernourished. They looked like the people I'd seen coming into the camp, who had no doubt joined the dead by now.

Another difference between us, was that he'd been wealthy. He'd had a big house, with far too many bedrooms considering the fact he, like me, had no siblings and even a holiday home further out on the coast, even though he hadn't been able to visit that since the war started. I, in contrast, had been living in a makeshift house, not even brick, like most of our village. We weren't uncivilized and we weren't living in the past; we were just poor, especially since the war had been on.

Even the big cities were struggling for rations, but the small towns like Ajka had no hope when things started running short. We had to rely on the things around us, whereas Jakob and his family could have bought things from the black market if they had been that way inclined.

So if this had seemed like a step down for me, it had likely been torture for Jakob when he came.

Apart from these things, our lives had been pretty generic. We'd made friends, lost friends, been to school, been engaged...

Just like I'd been meant to get married to Adrian, Jakob had had someone he was supposed to wed as well. Unlike me, who'd been thrilled that I got to spend the rest of my life with my best friend, someone I'd grown up with and trusted with my life, he'd been given to someone no more than a random stranger - something I'd always dreaded the idea of. Jakob hadn't been so enthusiastic about his betrothal.

I knew my father would never force someone I didn't want on me, which is why I'd ended up with Adrian, but Jakob hadn't been so lucky. Because his father was in such a big and important organisation, Jakob needed to be partnered with someone that could be trusted. A number of people outside of Abwehr could be spies, just worming there way in through an innocent boy who needed to be wed. So, that was why Jakob was engaged to one of the main conspirator's daughter. She was someone that wasn't likely to betray the cause. Also, Jakob knew that by giving his only child to the cause, his father was proving his loyalty. The decision was not at all regarding Jakob's happiness.

His father hadn't been so heartless as to say they must be wed instantly, deciding that his son should at least have the chance to know the girl he was supposed to spend the rest of his life with. Whilst this had been no help to Jakob, who had just realised that his future wife was stupid and annoying, someone who's company he could barely tolerate, the girl had, understandably, grown to love Jakob, who had never voiced his dislike.

At the end of the story, he'd finished with a rueful smile. "At first, the only good thing about coming to this place was leaving her."

Surely she couldn't have been that bad, and I'd thought that was quite mean until he carried on what he was saying, and informed me that I was the best thing that had happened at all, my heart fluttered, whilst I tried to conceal the fond smile that desperately wanted to spread across my face.

I might have felt bad for the girl, but when he said things like that, it was hard to remember why.

I smiled now, at the memory of it. I hoped he'd hurry up, it was getting cold out now and I needed his arms around me to take the chill away. My ragged sack wasn't much a shield against the cold and my bare legs and arms were littered with goose bumps.

When I saw a figure approaching out of the darkness, I grinned. Jakob was here.

I stood up, ready to embrace him, but that idea was cast out of my mind immediately when I realised that the man in front of me wasn't the officer I was expecting.

He was a similar height and girth, which was why I hadn't picked up on it straight away, but now I could see him getting closer, I picked out that he was a lot older and probably balding beneath the cap which adorned his head; straight, rather than askew like Jakob liked it.

Jolting backwards in panic, I raced towards the door of my hut, hoping that this man would just ignore me and not bother to waste his energy to question what I was doing.

Only, as I wrenched open the door of the hut, not caring if I woke up any number of my fellow hut-mates, a hand clamped down on my arm.

My immediate reaction was to open my mouth and let out a bloodcurdling scream. But I never got that far. As soon as my mouth parted and the beginning of a shriek brewed in the back of my throat, a second hand was smothering my face and cutting off any attempts at noise that I might have made.

That didn't mean I gave up, though. I started struggling, thrashing around violently in my captor's arms and refusing to settle, despite my quickly laboured breathing, due to the lack of good diet I'd had recently. I wasn't just lashing out aimlessly, though. I was trying to kick the side of the rickety building in front of me. I knew making a noise probably wouldn't benefit me in any way, not really, but it seemed the only choice I had.

Once again, my abductor knew what I was doing before I had time to accomplish it, however. I was wrenched back violently, away from the building when he realised that I could still reach things with my limbs.

"Don't even think about it." His rough German accent breathed in my ear, sending shivers down my spine as I squirmed in revulsion. On Jakob, a German accent was surprisingly attractive, but here, it just made me more anxious and afraid, though I tried my best not to show it.

I didn't submit to his grasp, though, and I continued my futile attempts at getting his hands off me, becoming more violent when his dark laughter reached my ears. The fact he was enjoying my resistance should have been warning enough for me to stop, but instinct didn't let me and I carried on fighting, regardless of the sensibility of it.

"A feisty one, I like it." His voice wasn't in my ear any more, but I could still hear it clear enough and I didn't like the hint of sadism that I caught in it. "Whoever's been fucking you must have liked it too."

That just made me struggle further and with a more desperate hopelessness as I realised exactly what he planned on doing with me. Jakob had warned me of this, that when people saw one person was being targeted, the others started to pick on her as well. He'd said he couldn't do that to me, but it had been worthless in the end anyway. The fact I was better fed, even marginally, than everyone else, had done it.

And I now, I was finally going to suffer what everyone else had to keep their lives around here.

It was all I deserved, really. I didn't earn the presidential treatment that Jakob gave me whilst everyone else suffered, so why shouldn't I have to endure the sexual abuse that should come with the extra food?

I tried to tell myself that I should just accept it, but my brain didn't listen and I continued to thrash mindlessly, using all my effort to break free.

It was hopeless, though, and there was no way I could get out of his iron grip.

"I think we should do this somewhere more private." His breath was back in my ear and I felt him lick the side of my neck.

I screamed out in disgust, but his hand swallowed it and nobody heard.

Then he was dragging me.

I thought back to when Stephánia had told the tale of her rape and wondered if mine would go the same. It had already been strikingly similar, and I wondered how often these men actually did this. There were enough candidates for their torment, and from what Jakob had told me, it appeared to be a relatively regular event. Stephánia had endured the abuse many a time after the first attack.

I'd stopped bothering to try escaping his arms by the time we reached his small, cramped bedroom, knowing that my attempts were futile and that I was just wasting my energy, which could be redirected later down the line.

As I'd been being dragged, I'd taken the time to actually look at my surroundings. Whilst I'd been here, the most I'd seen of the place we'd been being held was the rickety shacks that we were forced to live in and the copy's of our own, from where we went to work everyday and when we were taken to watch the rioting. I'd never seen the soldier's quarters before.

In all honesty, it wasn't that different to the places we were dwelling in. Whilst the buildings weren't actually falling down, they held the same grey feel about them. Like everything inside was completely evil - and it was rightly so, considering what was happening to me. It was one building, with lots of smaller rooms inside, like a barracks or dormitory.

The only good thing in them, was Jakob. But, he wouldn't hear me when this man was forcing himself on me, and I wouldn't want him to. I'd told him once that I wouldn't tell him if someone here raped me, and I planned on sticking by that. It would just make him feel incredibly guilty and there was no point in that. I'd hide it away and he'd never know.

He'd hate himself if he though he'd brought this upon me.

When we got to the anonymous officer's room, he let go of me and locked the door, just as Stephánia had described her rapist doing. From knowledge on her experience, I already knew what was hopeless, what was not and what to definitely not do - kick him in the most painful part. That had made it worse for her and I doubted it would be any different for me.

Instead, I just stood where he'd let go of me, in the middle of the confined area, with my arms folded defiantly whilst I tried desperately to stop the shaking that had taken over my body. When Stephánia had admitted to the abuse, I'd felt horrible for her, but of course I hadn't really understood. I didn't know what it felt like to be raped, and I still didn't. But, from the waiting, I began to get a feel of just how terrified she had actually been.

When the soldier finally turned around, I felt myself pale even more at the sight of his malicious grin and how his eyes raked over my scantily clad figure. He reached out, obviously planning to drag me closer to him, but I hopped out of the way at the last minute and tried desperately to think of something that might postpone this even a little bit longer.

"Wait," I ordered, trying to stop the obvious shaking in my voice. "Why are you doing this?" That was quite an open question, I might get minutes if I kept pushing it.

He paused, much to my relief, and looked at me curiously. "What do you mean?" He inquired, eyebrows furrowed.

I thought my question was quite clear in what I was asking, but I guess this man wasn't used to anything more than alarmed screams and shrieks from his other victims. "This." I gestured around the room, then at me. "Why do you want to hurt me?"

My voice had become marginally stronger as I realized that he was actually listening to what I was saying, rather than giving me a slap and pinning me to the bed. He hadn't even moved any closer to me.

His eyebrows knitted even further together when I clarified what I'd meant and he actually looked as though he didn't know the answer. He paused and scratched the greying stubble on his chin. "I don't know." He finally admitted. "I don't want to hurt you, exactly," he began. "I just want to please myself."

I knew he'd been genuine in his revelation, but it didn't take away from my shock. "That's really...selfish!" I accused, knowing that it was probably a mistake as soon as it exited my mouth. I'd decided I was trying to stall, not aggravate. Aggravating the man wasn't likely to do me any favours in the long run.

He laughed darkly. "And what else do you suggest? There's hardly many whores around for me to pick on, are there? Besides, what would I pay them with? Your hand gets boring after a while. So, young Jewish girls are my last resort." He explained, thinking that he was making a good point. "Young Jewish girls like you."

I could see him getting ready to move towards me again, so I blurted out the first thing that came into my head. "Couldn't you just go without?" I realized how stupid that sounded as soon as I'd said it, but it was a perfectly good point as far as I was concerned. Sex wasn't exactly mandatory to live.

"Go without?" The soldier asked incredulously, staring at me as though I was mad. "How many good things do you think there are her, girl? You've got to find pleasure where you can, and take, even if it's by force. Without something to look forward to, how else do you think we'd cope?"

I could actually see his logic, despite the atrocity of it. He was trying to make the best out of a bad situation, that I could understand. He was indulging himself where he could, that I could understand as well. What I couldn't quite get my head around, however, was how he could take an unwilling girl, always at least half his age, and force himself on her, knowing that it was hurting her and scarring her both mentally and physically.

"Doesn't it bother you, though? Don't you have even a little bit of remorse when you hear people screaming whilst you're hurting them?" I pushed, genuinely interested in his answer now. Whereas I'd only been buying time before, it was almost enlightening getting an insight into someone else's thought processes, especially when it was concerning something so despicable.

He weighed it over, then shook his head. "No." He replied blatantly. "No, I don't."

"How?"

He shrugged dismissively. "Think of it like this," he began. "Ever since I got here, I've had it drilled into my head that Jewish people are evil. You're going to overthrow the German rein, that you're trying to take over the world, that you'd be doing the same to us if you'd had the opportunity. Of course I thought that was verging on insane when I first heard it, but after a while it stuck, and now it's all I know. The first time I took a girl into my bed, she was horrified and she screamed the whole time, but I didn't even flinch. She was evil as far as I, and everyone else, was concerned. She deserved the pain."

I opened my mouth in horror. How could someone do that without feeling any guilt whatsoever. I felt guilty for the slightest things. "Surely not every officer does this?" I questioned instead of voicing my disgust, picking up on how he mentioned 'everyone else'.

Of course, I wasn't including Jakob in my 'everyone'. As much as I knew that, yes, Jakob was a German soldier working here, I couldn't quite bring myself to associate him with the others. When I looked at the man and thought of Jakob, there was no fathomable connection, other than their nationality and their jobs. Of course, I also doubted every soldier here was like the man in front of me, but it was the general impression that I got.

Jakob was a one-off, as far as I was concerned.

"Most." He stated. "In fact, yes, I'd have said nearly all of them, obviously there's a few exceptions. The weaklings that don't dare take what's theirs."

My face darkened as he indirectly insulted Jakob. "There not weak, they're brave, brave enough to do what they want instead of listening to the people spouting nonsense to get you to keep us captive here."

"You have a sharp tongue." The man said, not in an accusing tone, but more of an amused one. "Whoever picked you had good choice. Although, I can't quite understand why you didn't ask him all these questions rather than me."

I sighed. "Because there isn't a 'him'."

The officer rolled his eyes. "I'm not blind, girl. I can see that someone's been feeding you, everyone else in that damned hut of yours is stick and bones now." He reached out and I prepared to dodge backwards, but wall was the only thing I hit. He grabbed hold of my arm, and only my arm, much to my relief. "See, you've got more fat on you than anyone else in there."

I shook my head. "I was fatter than everyone else when I arrived." I lied. I don't know why I was so adamant on denying it, but it just seemed to be putting it off even longer. Having said that, there wasn't much point in putting off, it was going to happen anyway.

"You're telling lies, girl." He hissed. "No one could still be as big as you without having been given extra. Besides, I remember you from the lines.

You were a twiggy little thing back then as well. You've been given more than everyone else."

When he said that he recognised me, I made a point to study his features more closely. I'd been concentrating more on getting away from him than picking out whether or not I'd seen him before. But, now I was making a point to look, I realised that I had seen him before. He was the officer Jakob had been accompanying when we first arrived. He'd been behind the desk and had leered at me even then.

"Either that, or you've been stealing."

His accusation brought me back to the situation at hand and I blanched. "I haven't stolen anything." I defended myself. "Just because I haven't been...raped," I faltered over the word, "doesn't mean someone hasn't been giving me extra."

I didn't know why I had just admitted to that, but I didn't want to even indirectly accuse Jakob of hurting me. It was something hard to lie about even if he'd never find out.

"What craven is doing that? Does he think he's fattening you up or something? You're not a bloody chicken." I bit my lip to stop me saying something that would get me into even more trouble, something defending Jakob's honour. "Well, he's missed his chance now, hasn't he? I'm going to be the first to take you, you can gloat about that the next time you see your coward. What's he look like anyway, who is he?"

I cursed mentally. Who was he? Well, there was definitely another lie coming here. "He's...old, nearly forty, going grey, I don't know his name, he never told me." I lied, pausing between each detail a I tried to recreate the picture of a general officer's image.

"Sounds rather like me."

I flushed when I realized that I'd just, in affect, described the man in front of me. That hadn't been the idea, but, in all honesty, he was the typical picture I created of a soldier here.

"Yes," I agreed, reluctantly. "Kind of like you."

He snorted, but made no further effort to question me about it. "Well, I'm sure I'll recognize the anger in his face when you tell him what I did to you."

"And what if I don't tell him? Then you'll be disappointed." I remarked sarcastically.

The man in front of me regarded me as though I was mad. "And why would you do that? Don't you want him to hurt me, to be annoyed that I stole his prize?" He inquired, eyebrows furrowing much as they had when I'd first questioned him. "What do you think you'd be protecting him from?"

I glanced away. That was something I wasn't about to get into, especially not with someone who planned on doing something so atrocious to me. I wasn't going to give anyone an insight into what I was thinking.

Only, whilst I'd been refusing to answer that particular question, the soldier had come to a conclusion of his own; which wasn't too far off the mark. "You like him, don't you? You love him. You don't want him to abandon you when he realises there's nothing left for him to take from you."

Immediately, I shook my head. "You think that I could love someone who I knew was going to rape me?" I asked, incredulously, managing not to lie outright, but stay away from the person I knew Jakob to be.

"No, but you don't think he's going to hurt you, I can see it in your eyes. You think you've found your perfect protector, but it's all a lie. He's just wants to fuck someone when they want it, without the screams of pain that come with it. It's all a farce, you'll see that soon enough."

I refused to believe that what he was saying had any bearing of truth and that clearly came across in my facial expression. Jakob wouldn't do that, what would be the point? He could take every single girl in this camp to his bed until he found one that wanted to have sex with him, what reason would he have to single me out for that? It was trial and error if that really was the game he was playing.

Having said that, I still wasn't sure why he'd bothered with me in the first place. I wasn't exactly special when it came to my appearance, or my personality.

"That's not true." I denied fervently, not giving him the satisfaction of seeing even the niggling of doubt forming in my mind. "You don't know anything."

"Well, at least you've stopped denying that you love him now."

"I don't love him."

Did I? I wasn't sure. How could you determine between like and love? I definitely cared about Jakob a lot, but did that mean I loved him? I didn't know for certain.

The phrase 'you don't know what you've got until it's gone' popped into mind and I wondered if my feelings really would only become clear at that moment - which was inevitably going to come.

"Dumme schlampe," He muttered in German, uttering something I had no chance of understanding.

That brought me back to something else someone had recently said to me in German that I hadn't understood. Sensing that it would be better to ask my random assaulter than Jakob, where I might embarrass myself for having not known it in the first place, I took my opportunity.

"Do you know what ich liebe dich means?" I inquired, knowing I'd pronounced the words badly.

The officer gave me a puzzled look, and I sighed. He wasn't going to tell me.

"It means I love you."

I felt my face freeze and the heat rise to my cheeks as I thought back to the sincerity in Jakob's voice and face when he'd said it.

He'd said he loved me.

I felt the smile rising on my face, despite the dire situation and I bit my lip to stop me breaking out into a full blown grin.

Then, I was brought back to reality with a jerk as the soldier in front of me finally made his move. He grabbed my arm and pulled me with a sudden movement towards him.

My face paled with panic when I realised that my stalling was at an end. "Tell your lost German love about this the next time you see him." He rasped, dragging me so that I was forced to be pressed completely up against him.

Whilst I'd managed to control my struggling when being hauled here, because I'd come to the conclusion he wouldn't actually do anything until we reached his room, this was entirely different. Now I knew what was about to happen and my automatic reaction was to throw all my might into getting away from him.

Not that it was any more successful this time.

His hands ran over all my body despite my very vocal and physical protests. Now that we had reached the confines of his room, there was no reason to stop my screaming and shouting, and I didn't hold back.

I shouted, hit and kicked, whilst he grabbed my hips, my breasts, my thighs. Revulsion was the only emotion I could comprehend as I continued to struggle.

"I said I liked them feisty." He muttered against my ear, his breath tickling my neck as I felt the bile rise in the back of my throat. "I'll definitely be having you again."

Then he released me, and I felt the slightest twinge of relief. From his words mere seconds ago, I should have realised that it was premature and he was just preparing for what was to come. He was pulling his trousers down.

I backed away from him, making sure to avoid looking at his newly visible arousal, but the wall was the only place left for me to go. I pressed up against it regardless and felt the tears accumulating in my eyes. The reality was setting in and I knew that it was going to be a thousand times worse than I could imagine.

And then it would happen again.

And again, and again, if what he'd said was anything to go by.

A tear slipped out of my eye and travelled down my cheek when the soldier appeared in my vision once more. His hands grasped my arms so tight I knew I would have bruises by the morning.

I was already up against the wall, but that didn't dissuade him from shoving even closer. My head banged against the solid surface and I felt my vision blur for a moment, but I restrained from crying out in pain. He wouldn't get that much satisfaction, even though I doubted he'd noticed the force at which he'd shunted me.

This time when he ran his hands up my thighs, he brought the dress with him and held it around my hips so that he could access what he wanted.

I didn't give up, though. He wouldn't take me easily, that was for sure.

I shoved with all of my weight, I slapped his face with all my force, but he didn't even flinch. He just got the same sadistic quality to his expression again and with disgust, I realised that I was just enticing him even more.

I still kicked and thrashed, but he soon got tired of it and grabbed my wrists in his. He pinned them above my head with one of his hands and left the other free, to trail down my body.

Gagging as he pinched my nipple with an excessive force, he quickly left it alone and carried on his path. I writhed and squirmed, but it just caused him to push closer against me and press his hardness against the area I dreaded it touching the most.

The shoved his knee between mine, which I'd clamped together with as much force as possible, and used his free hand to grab a thigh. Then, he pried my legs open, so that I was in a vulnerable position, where he had access to everything.

Leaning forward to whisper in my ear once more, I found myself shaking with fear. "Where's your precious German saviour now?"

That was when the shot went off and the blood began to spurt from the officer's mouth as he slumped forward, his body going instantly limp.

"Here I am."

Eventually, yes I have uploaded! I've had this in my head for ages and these next few chapters are the penultimate ones. It's getting near the end of the story now, but I already know how it's going to end! It should be good ;D

Hope this chapter was alright, and no, I didn't make her suffer the same fate as Stephania, I'm not that harsh. And, Jakob to the rescue! Of course he was going to turn up sooner or later!

Hope this chapter was okay and sorry for the long wait, I am going to be getting back to a more regular schedule from now on. I really want to get this story finished now :)

And the song is AMAZING. I don'ti even like Oasis that much, but this song is just really catchy.

Thanks to all the votes and comments, they are muchly appreciated!

Chapter Fourteen

- -

Chapter Fourteen...

I stared in horror at the body now slumped against me, then at Jakob's pale face and the shaky hand that had dropped his gun in shock.

It took us both several moment's to snap back into reality, but then we knew that we had to get out of there. I shoved the officer's body away from me with all my force and staggered forwards, where Jakob instantly reached out to steady me.

"We need to leave." I said, sounding almost half-asleep as I took in the scene around me. Blood was smothered across the floor, still leaking from the soldier's back flowing to where he'd had me pinned against the wall.

Jakob was white as a sheet and visibly shaking from as the impact of what he'd just done began to settle in and he realised he'd just killed a man.

He nodded, also not quite conscious as he responded. "We'll go back to my room, it's not far from here." He agreed, grabbing hold of my arm and leading me outside. "If we see anyone, pretend to struggle. That won't look abnormal. Walking so easily will." He advised, explaining in not so many words why he had a hold of my arm, even if it was gentle.

Clumsily, I let him guide me out of the room. I could feel the tension in his grip, but I knew he was trying to gain some composure as we walked. I had an excuse to look hysterical, I was supposedly being led off to be raped, but Jakob had to look normal. Stern. Strict. Like the German soldier that he was.

He managed it surprisingly well.

I was much the opposite.

Each doorway we passed, I flinched, thinking I was going to have to put on some kind of performance and that I'd fail and give the game away. But, each doorway we passed, no one came out to surprise me.

I had no doubt that the gunshot must have been heart throughout most of the building, but it was obviously a more common sound that I assumed, because whilst I'd expected people to be running around manically, searching for the murderer who was on a rampage going round killing people, everything was just as it was when I came down here.

Quiet and filled with a sense of dread.

When we reached his room without incident, I couldn't help the breath of relief that escaped my lips. We'd made it this far unscathed, which whilst wasn't must of an achievement in the scheme of things, boded well for a future without being caught. At least now we had time to talk about what had happened, before everything went predictably wrong.

Shutting the door behind him, Jakob sat down on his bed and ran a hand through his hair, not even glancing at me, but staring at his gun hand in horror.

Awkwardly, I stood watching him, not sure what I could do and wondering if any soothing gestures I made would be taken offensively or as comfort. Deciding I might as well risk rejection, I tentatively sat down next to him and rested a hand on his arm, glancing at him unsurely.

He returned my gaze, but neither had any words of comfort for the other. What was there to say? It wasn't going to be okay, so that soothing phrase was out of the question. Filling up on false hope wasn't going to help at all.

I rested my head on his shoulder when my hand wasn't rebuffed and savoured the feeling of his arm, which quickly wrapped around my shoulder. "I can't believe he almost raped you." Jakob's voice was livid when he said that and I saw his fist clench so hard that his knuckles turned white. "He almost took you and I only just got there in time. One second later and he'd have already done it."

I grasped his arm tighter and tried to stop the tears accumulating in my eyes. I was determined not to look back on that now. There was no point traumatising myself with memories when there was plenty of things in the present that demanded my attention.

Not that they were much better.

"You killed him." I whispered, still not quite believing the words that came out of my mouth. That Jakob had pulled the trigger on someone. And despite the appalled look on his face at what he'd just done when I first laid eyes on him, I'd seen the pure rage in his eyes and the sweet satisfaction at having hurt someone who hurt me.

"I didn't mean to." He responded, shaking his head. "I just saw him and he had you up against the wall and he was going to..." He trailed off and I saw his jaw tighten. "It was the first thing I thought to do. I grabbed, aimed, and pulled."

I traced a pattern on his arm and tried to thing of something so say that comforted him that soothed, while didn't encourage him, but all that I could manage to utter was a meagre "thank you."

He tried to smile, but his face only twisted into a further grimace. "I don't regret it." He finally stated. "I feel like I should. I've just shot a man for god's sake, but I'd rather that than let him touch you again."

"I know. I'm just sorry you had to do it." I whispered softly.

"That's the first time I've ever pulled that trigger." He informed me ruefully. "But I'm glad I shot one of them rather than one of you."

"Me too."

I didn't feel like I was really offering him much, with my simple answers, but nothing else was coming into my mind. What was I supposed to say to all of this? It had happened and nothing could undo that. As far as I was concerned, Jakob had had all the right reactions during the aftermath and I couldn't fault his logic at all.

I just hoped it wouldn't come back to haunt him eventually. He was clearly already suffering, but I longed that it would get better rather than worse. If Jakob started becoming traumatised over this, then I'd have to cope for us both, and that wouldn't be fun.

"What do we do now, Jakob?" I asked, my voice far too feeble and worried for my liking.

"We wait." He decided, sounding much calmer and in control than I did. "If we're lucky, nothing will come of it. They might just dismiss it as an accident and let it blow over. Everything will go back to normal soon." He tried to reassure the both of us.

I bit my lip, unconvinced. "But what if it doesn't? What will happen then?"

"We'll get to that when we come to it," he muttered. "It's something I don't even want to consider."

I sighed. "Fair enough." I agreed, knowing that he was right. The consequences if people found out about this for Jakob would be torturous. He would be subject to everything his father went through and more. I couldn't bare to think about that either, so I blocked out further thoughts from my subconscious and stuck to the present once more. The future wasn't something I wanted to dwell on either.

There was another prospect I was also trying to avoid contemplate, though. What would happen to me if Jakob was caught out?

Would I be blamed for it? I was the reason Jakob had shot the soldier after all, but no one else would know that, not really. Jakob certainly wouldn't mention my name at all, not that anyone would expect him to know it, so anything they did would be based on presumption.

It didn't matter why they did it as long as they did though. Anything they did to me was going to be bad, no matter what the reasons were.

Jakob might have shot one person to stop them raping me, but he couldn't shoot the entirety of the officers placed here when they found me here and took me by force.

"Thank you." I repeated my earlier sentiments, feeling as though I needed to reiterate my gratitude. "I owe you my life."

"I didn't save your life." He pointed out.

I smirked. "I owe you my virtue, then." I joked, trying to sound happy, but failing miserably so that we both knew my heart wasn't in it.

He also attempted a grin back, but we both knew it didn't reach his eyes and the apprehension was hanging heavy in the air. His arm tightened around me and I leaned further into him, finding his embrace more comforting than any words he could give me.

He kissed my forehead gently and rested his head on top of my own, not having the effort left to do anything else.

We didn't know what was going to happen, we didn't know what was going to happen. But, there was nothing we could do, until it did.

We just had to wait.

Turns out we didn't have to wait long, though.

Someone knocked on the door and both mine and Jakob's faces paled. "What do we do?" I hissed in a whisper.

He looked at me guilty and then grabbed a hold of my hips. "Struggle." He ordered. "Look at me with as much hate as you can muster. After all, I'm about to rape you."

I panicked. How was I supposed to pretend to be terrified of Jakob? Being terrified of the officers outside, that would be much easier.

The door opened when Jakob didn't respond and I glanced at the two soldiers in the doorway wide-eyed. They were polar opposites when it came to their appearances. The first was short and stout, his face round, eyes slits between the overly fleshy skin. The second was tall and thin, his with a long face and clearly defined features, which included a hooked nose and thin lips.

But, whilst their appearances were completely contrary to the other's, I could tell by their expressions that there personalities consisted of the same basic qualities. They were both sleazy and cruel.

"Office Eichel." The one on the left addressed him with a cool courtesy. "Don't stop on our account." He taunted, his face smug as his eyes raked over my scantily clad body.

I saw the muscle in Jakob's cheek jump, but he managed not to snap an insult at the two men. "I prefer not having an audience." He retorted, still keeping what appeared to be a possessive hold on my waist.

I squirmed, forcing my eyes to fill up with tears as I tried to get away from who the men would assume to be my abuser. Jakob glared at me and I froze, trying to act like a deer caught in the headlights.

"But she looks so terrified." The second soldier sneered, his eyes appraising my figure once more.

Jakob sent them such a venomous glare that I actually shrunk back against the bed, further away from him than I'd already been putting on. "It's none of your business though, is it?" He replied, clenching his jaw and refraining from saying anything more.

"We have reason to believe otherwise."

My face, if possible, became ever deathlier pale and I flinched despite myself. That couldn't possibly mean what I thought it meant, could it?

"Why, what's happened? Has raping innocent girls suddenly become a crime? As far as I was concerned, I thought it was more of a sport around here."

His voice was thick with anger and he was unflinching as he addressed them, but I could feel the tension in his body, which was pressed against mine.

Despite the fact he was supposedly about to rape me, I took solace in the feeling of flesh against flesh and I knew that I would be even more of a shaking wreck if it wasn't for his presence.

"Someone was shot." The first officer explained, his chin quivering with each word that he spoke. "So we're going through every room until we find out who it was."

"What makes you think it was an officer. Couldn't it have been someone he was…amusing, that stole his gun, or something?" He inquired, feigning ignorance to make him seem less of a suspect.

And to be fair, it was a good point that he made.

But, the second officer shot him down immediately. "The soldier still had his gun on him, a second gun was left on the floor." My eyes widened when I realised that Jakob had left his gun. Now he was done for. How was he going to escape the fact that his gun was missing. "Plus, he was shot in the back. No one could do that when being raped."

The way he said it was in the crude manner that the officer Jakob had shot had had. Neither of them were anything other than blunt and offensive. They held none of the caution Jakob had when he was around me, so as not to offend anyone.

"Well, I don't know what you expect me to have done. I'm clearly occupied." He put his hand on my breast as a show of what they'd supposedly interrupted and despite the surprising wave of pleasure I felt, I squeaked and squirmed, pretending that I wanted to get away from him no matter what the costs.

"The soldier had his cock out when we found him." Office number one remarked.

"We think you shot him and ran off with his whore." Office number two accused.

Both of their gazes bored into Jakob and he struggled to think of something to come back with.

"I've been here the whole time." I spoke up, my voice wobbling nervously.

I knew I shouldn't have said anything, that I'd just be making this worse for myself if it backfired, but I had to try. I was a girl who was underneath him, about to be defiled by this monster. I'd have no reason to be defending him unless I was telling the truth.

The two officers in the doorway directed their attention solely at me now and I struggled not to shrink away under their scrutiny. I could hardly get closer to Jakob without it looking suspicious, like I would have done otherwise, so leaning further into the bed was the most I could do to put space between me and the officers.

They did something I hadn't expected, though. Instead of just leaving and accepting the fact Jakob had been abusing me the entire time, going to question one of the other thousands of officers instead, they pointed a finger at me. "Up," the first ordered. "Get up and come over here."

I hesitated, but had no choice but to obey. Jakob was reluctant to move so that I could leave the bed, but he had no other option. If he wanted to get out of this alive, then he had to submit to their requests, even if that was with a certain amount of arrogance.

Tentatively, I stood up, shaking on my legs as I stumbled forward slightly. Unlike Jakob, who would have instantly reached out to stabilise me, the two men just shared a smug smirk with each other.

When the first officer did reach out, it was to pull me roughly towards him, rather than to help me. Turning me around and letting the other officer take a hold of my other arm, I was suspended between them.

After glancing at Jakob and taking in his livid facial expression, I turned my gaze to the floor. I wasn't going to look like I was staring at him for help. I felt a hand on my waist, and hand on my bum, a hand fondling my breast and I held back a retch.

The second officer pinched my nipple with a painful amount of force and I couldn't help but cry out as he dug his nails in.

Jakob was up in a flash, but stopped when the officer let go and pulled out the fabric, holding it out for everyone to see. "A blood splatter?" He inquired, sarcastically. "But where could a blood splatter have come from when you've been here with officer Eichel the whole time?"

I paled and struggled to come up with a plausible excuse. "It's old." I lied. "From dismantling the glasses." I held out my hands, a mixture of scars and new cuts from this day and the last. "I always cut myself."

The first officer snorted. "But that doesn't explain the absence of officer Eichel's gun, now, does it?"

They'd planned it all, I realised then. By pulling me up, hurting me, they knew Jakob would spring up from his laid down position and give his empty holster away. They couldn't just ask him to show them his holster and then take him in, I didn't know. They obviously enjoyed giving me the false hope that I might be able to help Jakob escape this unscathed.

Either way, it would have reached the same end conclusion.

As it was, they'd just managed to amuse themselves more in the process.

Whilst I was staring at Jakob in horror, suddenly knowing that this was the end for us, that we'd both been tricked into giving ourselves away.

Jakob had revealed his missing gun and I'd lied. I'd lied about being here the whole time, which meant I'd defied their command and subject myself to death.

It was all going awfully wrong for us.

I failed to miss the hand that was groping for my thigh again until it had grasped a hold of it and I had tumbled sideways into the second soldier. He took advantage of that immediately and wrapped an arm around my waist, his hand trailing upwards until it reached my breast.

His hand tangled in my hair and forced my head backwards. "And now I'm going to f*ck you whilst he watches." He said against my throat, loud enough for everyone in the room to hear.

Jakob released a primal noise that sounded almost a growl when he leapt forward, punching the officer who had hold of me right in the face.

He released his grasp instantly so that he could cradle his nose and I stumbled forward into Jakob, who was breathing heavily and muttering a string of German expletives under his breath.

Jakob didn't hesitate before shoving me behind him protectively. The two officers had both reached the same conclusion as they sobered up, however, and both had their guns pointing straight at Jakob, more than prepared to pull the trigger if he made a move to harm them again.

"You don't need to shoot me." Jakob stated, his voice rough with anger. "And you don't need to hurt her either."

"And why shouldn't we? We've clearly discovered that it annoys the hell out of you."

"Because this isn't a case for people as low down as you," I could see both of their faces darken at that thinly veiled insult and I prayed that Jakob knew what he was doing. "This needs to go to the top of command. What will he say if he knows you've spoiled a young girl whilst trying to annoy me. He might want the honour of that himself. Then you'd have gotten yourselves in a mess, wouldn't you?"

His taunts were merciless and I felt myself pale at the mention of whoever was in charge having a go at me himself, but I knew this was just Jakob trying to stall, as I had done with the dead officer. Time, even a little of it, was better than nothing.

The two officers exchanged thoughtful looks, before nodding.

"Fair enough." The first man agreed reluctantly. "We'll take you to the commander. And then we'll give your girl to every soldier in this place and you can watch them rape her."

Ah, after the relief of her escaping the last man, I feel rather guilty for this. But, I've had it all planned out for ages now and I know exactly how it's going to go! And, on the positive side, I uploaded quickly! An achievement in itself!

Thanks for all the votes and comments, I got up to #28 on the Historical Fiction what's hot! Amazing to me!

Hope I'm not making this turn out too dark or gloomy for anyone, but I feel it's how it would have been for the people living there, if not much worse. I can't write about the time period and make it seem like it was full of smiles and rainbows. I'm trying to make it as realistic as possible. I hope no one's disappointed by that!

Hope you enjoyed this chapter, and I'll be uploading soon.

After all, less than five chapters left, I think! :(

And I think the song fits, for once, it's not just one I've randomly selected :P

Chapter Fifteen

Chapter Fifteen...

I shuddered as I passed through the door and under the arm of officer number one who was holding it open for me. His short stature meant I came a lot closer to him than I would have liked, but there was the small victory when he didn't reach out and grab me like I'd been expecting.

I figured that was mainly because Jakob had been right behind me, however.

When we started walking down the corridor, the two officers walked in front, leaving Jakob and I to lag behind as much as we dared without being picked up on it and forced to walk at gunpoint, like I doubted they'd have any qualms in doing.

A couple of minutes later and we finally dared to converse with each other, if only in snippets, our voices so low we could barely hear the other. "We're going to die." I said bluntly, hoping that if I said it out loud then the concept would become easier to understand, rather than just being something I was failing to comprehend properly. It was all too surreal.

Jakob looked very much like he wanted to disagree, but in the end he just nodded. "Yes, we are." He agreed glumly.

Suddenly, I remembered something that I'd meant to say when we went back to his room earlier. "I love you too." I blurted, my voice still quiet, but loud enough to convey how much I meant by the words.

His eyes widened and he looked at me with a sudden spark of happiness. "Really?" He whispered, the smile on his face giving me a rare moment of solace before the darkness that followed. "I didn't think you understood what I'd said."

"I didn't." I admitted. "But it turned out the dead soldier was good for something, at least."

I saw Jakob's expression threatening to darken, but he stopped it at the last second, not wanting to ruin the moment with curses to the dead man and his attempts at hurting me. "So that's why he said where's your German soldier now." He mused. "I didn't think you could have told him about me."

"I'm not that foolish." I told him seriously. "Although I feel like I should have just said Én is szeretlek, just to confuse you more."

Jakob smirked, an expression I hadn't seen often on his lips, but one that suited him just as much as everything else seemed to. "I could speak German at you all day and you'd only understand half of it." He reminded me. "But I don't understand any Hungarian. I'm guessing it means I love you too?"

I nodded. "Precisely." I confirmed.

"I wish I could kiss you." He suddenly said, glancing at the guards ahead of us as the reason why he hadn't just done it anyway. "I wish I could show you how much I mean it."

"I don't need you to show me." I told him honestly. "I already know, by everything you've done for me."

"I just wish there was someway I could save you from this. I won't let them touch you. I won't let them defile you like that. They have can every single girl in here, but not you."

Part of me wanted to tell him how selfish that had been. That he should care more about the majority and not just me. The other half wanted to swoon with joy that someone could possibly care that much and kiss him senseless.

Both parts stayed within my mind though and I just chose not to respond to his comment, simply looking at him with eyes that would tell him everything.

Suddenly, a thought struck me. In the first place, Jakob had been taken in as a soldier for not showing the betrayal his father had. Maybe he could save himself again. Maybe it wasn't the simple 'we're both going to die' after all.

I glanced at him sideways and noticed the determined expression on his face. He was prepared to die. He hadn't considered this like me and was just waiting for the bullet through his skull. Only this time, he didn't look concerned about it. When he talked about betraying his father, he always looked guilty, but his sheer fear of death was what had kept him from dying with him.

This time, he wasn't afraid. He was ready. He'd accepted his fate.

I wasn't ready to accept it for him, though.

I'd fight for him if I could.

"Jakob," I murmured softly. "I want you to promise me something."

He gazed upon my face with his chiselled features and I found myself breathless for a moment, just drinking in his beauty. I'd never really had the time to appreciate it before, but now I knew this was one of the last chances I might get to see his face as such as close proximity again, I made sure to commit every inch of his face to memory.

I stared into his friendly grey eyes and noticed only now that they had flecks of green running through them. They seemed to smile at me and that was more comforting than anything else I'd known during my stay here.

Then, I moved onto his nose. It wasn't perfect, but who's is? It had a soft ridge that raised just between the eyes then dropped to a soft button at the end. In a moment of absurdity, I urged to run my finger down it.

His mouth came next, and unlike his nose, that was perfect. His lips were neither a thin, hardly identifiable line, or overly voluptuous so they looked abnormal, but somewhere in the middle. They were full and perfect for kissing - like I'd experienced more than a few times. They were currently curved upwards into a small smile, which, like his eyes, soothed me some- what.

His hat was covering his hair, but I could see the short sweeping bit of mousy brown that covered his forehead and the trimmed sideburns which protruded from underneath the hat to barely reach the middle of his ear. His hat itself was set askew on his head, a quirky habit which allowed me to identify with him as a separate person to the rest of the clones who all talked and acted the same, despite their variety of appearances.

The awry positioning of his hat was the one thing that gave away the streak of defiance in him that I loved so much.

Bringing my thoughts back to my original speech and my eyes back to his own, he voiced an answer. "Anything."

"Promise me you'll do all you can to save yourself."

Unlike his vow of anything only seconds ago, any hint of a smile vanished from his lips with that. "Viktória..." He trailed off, unsurely. I could see the indecision in his eyes, but almost immediately I knew which choice he'd pick. "I can't promise you that."

I sighed, having realised before I asked that would be what he replied with. "You can." I assured him gently. "I want you to save yourself. I'm lost anyway, you know that, but you aren't. Not yet. You can stay alive. The war will be over soon and if you're lucky, then the German's won't win and this place will be closed down. You can go back to living a normal life." I tried to get him fantasising.

It worked and he closed his eyes momentarily, trying to picture the scene I'd created. "I want that." He admitted, smiling softly as he imagined. "But I want that with you, and it can't happen."

The illusion broke and his eyes reopened.

"It can," I tried to tell him desperately. "You can find someone else, you'll have forgotten about me soon enough."

He shook his head. "No." He stated resolutely. "I betrayed the only person I loved last time I had this decision, I won't be doing that again."

"Please," I begged. "Please don't die because of me."

He glanced at me. "I won't be dying because of you." He assured me. "I'll be dying because it's time for that, because I shot a man who was supposed to be on my side. I'll be dying because I chose to protect you, not because of you."

I paused, trying helplessly to think of some other argument. None came to me though and I resorted to just looking at him pleadingly, willing him to understand what I wanted and to accept that he might be able to get out of this alive if he played his cards right.

"And they'll ask me to hurt you." He said, ignoring my stare and further explaining his reasoning. "They won't just let me go like last time. They'll make me prove my worth. I'll have to hurt you. I don't know how, but I will. That's the only way I'll get to live."

"I don't care." I responded immediately. I already knew that I was in for a painful death and lots of unpleasant experiences, but if I knew it was for a purpose, for Jakob to live, it would become slightly more bearable. "I don't care what you'd have to do to me."

Jakob let out an aggravated sigh. "That's because you don't understand!" He whispered harshly. "I've seen what they do to people, you've seen what they do to people. What if they ask me to rape you?" He inquired, looking at me pointedly. "What if they ask me to kill you slowly. Shoot you in the foot, take you in the arm, then let you bleed to death. That could be hours worth of unbearable pain. You think I could do that to you? Just because I'm selfish enough to live."

I tried not to flinch. That didn't sound pleasant and I obviously didn't want that to happen to me. But, it was more than likely going to be my fate anyway. "And what do you think will happen if you don't?" I asked seriously. "You think they'll just shoot me in the head and let me have an instant death? They'll do exactly the same. You heard what they said. I'll have every soldier in the place taking me before your eyes. Do you think that's any better?"

His face darkened and his fist clenched. "Don't, Viktória." He warned.

"Don't what? Tell you the truth because you don't want to hear it?"

"Don't." He repeated, the muscle in his cheek jumping uncontrollably and his jaw clenching so tightly I was surprised he'd managed to speak.

"I want you to promise me you'll do everything you can to stay alive."

"I can't do that." He denied frantically. "I can't hurt you any more than I have already."

"The only thing you've done to hurt me is not make this promise." I told him, with part honesty. Whilst it was true, Jakob had never hurt me once, not making the promise didn't hurt me either. He was trying to be kind, he was trying to save me the trauma of being hurt by the person I loved, I couldn't be offended by his kindness.

I also knew that he couldn't admit to himself that I was right. If Jakob didn't do the things they asked of him, they would happen to me anyway, just with more people, being more violent and uncaring. I'd rather know that I was being hurt for a good reason.

"I promise."

Jakob's words caught me unawares and my eyes snapped to his, wide with surprise. "Really?" I whispered, needing to make sure I was hearing this right.

He nodded solemnly, looking less than pleased by that admission. "Really." He agreed. "I promise I'll do everything I can to stay alive."

I wasn't sure how that would go when it came down to it, but at least having that to fall back on was better than nothing. "Thank you." I replied, feeling the tears creep up on me, knowing that I was going to die no matter what. It was something that wasn't hard to accept, but it was a hell of a lot easier knowing that Jakob had the chance to do the opposite.

In a moment of bravery, he reached over and gave me the quickest peck on the mouth anyone could have imagined. It was so soft I found myself imagining if it had really happened, but it was more than enough to assure me I was doing the right thing. Jakob meant more to me than anything now, his life was worth a lot more than mine.

Then, I decided I had one last thing to ask of him. "Could you look out for Stephánia for me, if you do get out of this?"

His face twisted and I knew he was trying to let me down gently. "Viktória, I can't stop-"

I cut him off. "I know you can't stop her abuse and I know you can't stop what's happening to her family. I know you can't do anything for her really, it would just mean a lot if I knew you were watching out for her. You could keep her company, do something to make it seem less worse for her that I'm not there anymore."

Jakob nodded. "I'll do my best." He assured me.

"Thank you."

When we realised we had arrived at our destination, our wide eyes met in a final gaze. "I love you." Jakob repeated, sounding both glad and heartbroken he got to say that one more time.

I tried to smile, but it was watery and a tear, which I saw his hand itching to wipe away tenderly, slipped down my face. "I love you too." I responded almost silently, before officer number one had grabbed my arm and wrenched me away from Jakob, to throw me down in front of a man sat behind a big desk, where I fell to my knees and hung my head.

For the first time, I took a moment to look around the room we'd unknowingly entered. Compared to the two rooms I'd seen so far inside the building, this was a big contrast. The big desk the man in charge sat behind was piled high with papers, but seemed oddly organised despite that. There was no bed, but a smaller door on the other side of the room I presumed led to a bedroom.

There were other things that had been missing from the other people's rooms as well, though. A small television was placed in the corner, mounted on a side table which faced his desk. I'd only ever seen one television before, and that was the one we had in Ajka. It was owned by the richest family in the village, but they weren't selfish with it and people always gathered around there when something important was being broadcast.

There was a big wireless in the corner that was playing music softly. It wasn't really right for the mood though and it wasn't long before someone had turned it off. The relaxing classical music wasn't right for this kind of meeting.

It was easy to pick out that the man in question was important just by the way he looked. Whilst his actual features were normal, him being in the range of forty to fifty years of age, with a trim figure and neatly combed hair, his stance and outfit determined his status.

He was sat up straight and looked like he'd never slouched in his life. His hands were clasped in front of him professionally as he reviewed the people before him with his eyes. He wasn't wearing a hat and his hair was combed to perfection atop his head, despite the clear thinning of it and the grey streaks that were slowly overtaking his previous black hair. The clothes he wore were crisp and lush, still being soldier's garments, but adorned with several medals and not a crease in sight.

The lieutenant barked something out in German to the two men who were each holding Jakob by an arm each. They balked and I saw Jakob conceal a smile at their paling faces. It was in that moment that I realised just how much Jakob had accepted the fact he was as good as gone. He wasn't even bothering to respect this man who was clearly superior to all of them.

The first officer replied also in German, but his voice wasn't nearly as strong as it had been when taunting and threatening me. It was nervous, because he was scared of the power this man had over him.

Jakob snorted and hissed something out in his native tongue, which earned him a slap around the face and a knee in the gut from each of his captors. He spat out a glob of blood, but the sardonic smirk stayed on his face and I knew he was pleased that he'd aggravated them so easily.

It annoyed me that I couldn't understand what they were saying and I felt my eyes go wide and tears prick at corners of them when they struck Jakob, but the only noticeable reaction I gave was a flinch.

They switched to English then, for my benefit. "So, Officer Eichel, it appears you've got yourself a lady friend." He taunted, leering shamelessly at me. I winced and struggled back to my feet, not wanting to look so weak, despite knowing that was all I was.

As soon as I'd stood up again, though, I'd been forced roughly back down to my knees and I had to put my hands out to stop my head hitting the ground. My knees were grazed against the coarse concrete of the floor and the healing cuts on my hands split open again until they were dripping blood against the ground.

"She means nothing to me." Jakob spat, finally doing what I'd hoped and denying any kind of emotion towards me.

The lieutenant raised a sarcastic eyebrow at him and I knew he was an arrogant man. He had no sense of sincerity and I knew why he was in charge here. Someone with no other emotions than self-importance was exactly the type of man needed to run this kind of establishment. He didn't care who he hurt and how he did it as long as he wasn't harmed in the process. "But that doesn't explain why you protected her so much." He reminded Jakob.

"She's my possession." He stated blatantly. "I was feeding her up, I wanted to be the one to fuck her senseless when she was ready."

I winced, but didn't dare move again. If I didn't know better, I'd have said Jakob meant every word that came out of his mouth. He sure sounded convincing and the niggling of doubt at the back of my mind knocked my confidence in him somewhat. What if he had just been stringing me on for his own amusement? I didn't know him at all except for what he'd told me. He could have lied his way through the last couple of weeks and I wouldn't have known any better.

What if I'd made a complete fool of myself?

Then I reminded myself of all the risks he'd put himself under just for this. He wouldn't be here right now if this was all just a game to him. He wouldn't risk his life for a little entertainment.

And it all seemed so real. Even if Jakob was stringing me along, I couldn't deny my love for him now, it was as real as the scene playing out before me.

"Is that really worth killing a man for?" The lieutenant inquired, glancing at him with narrowed eyes, but an otherwise serene face.

"Yes." Jakob answered immediately. "He was stealing my prize, so I stole his life. It seemed like a fair trade to me."

The lieutenant gave a rasping laugh, which the two officers who were still holding Jakob joined in with nervously. When they received a harsh glare from the lieutenant though, they shut up immediately. "You do not shoot your brothers." He warned Jakob, his tone dangerous.

Despite knowing Jakob must have picked up on it, though, he was just as callous with his response. "You do not steal your brother's possessions." He replied bitterly.

"You share with your brothers." The lieutenant's response was immediate, as if he already knew what Jakob was going to shoot back at him.

Jakob was unfazed though and his face was still stony. "Not without asking first."

An amused smile set itself onto the man in charge's face then. "And tell me, Officer Eichel, if the dead man in question had come up to you and asked you pleasantly if he could rape this beautiful young woman here, would the outcome have been any different?"

Jakob smirked, still not accepting the fact he was backed into a corner. "Probably not." He admitted. "But at least then you'd have the point I shot him for no reason, as it is, I had a purpose."

I bit back a sudden burst of laughter. In the face of death, Jakob had definitely gained some courage, and whilst it might only be sealing his fate, he was doing well in making himself look brave and unconcerned. I was proud of him.

The lieutenant let out another grating laugh, louder this time, but the two officers had learnt their lesson and held their tongues. "You've got some balls you." The lieutenant remarked. "I think I might give you a promotion."

I tried not to let the relief show on my face. This was what I'd wanted, this was what I'd hoped for. Jakob was going to survive. He was going to survive and get a better position. I was still basking in liberation when he spoke again.

"But first you must prove your loyalty, although I guessed you'd already figured that out." He said, which Jakob made no response to. "Let him go, boys." He told the two officers, who dropped his arms immediately and took a wary step back to make sure Jakob couldn't strike them as payback for his earlier abuse.

Then, he threw Jakob the gun from his own holster, which Jakob caught effortlessly. Despite me never associating him with the other soldiers, it was only now that I remembered he had been trained as a boy to wield a gun and shoot people. There was no doubt that he was a killing machine, I'd just never thought about it before.

Weighing it over in his hand, he held it, finger on the trigger and aimed it at the second officer, the one who'd threatened to rape me whilst Jakob watched. The soldier shrunk back like a scared little boy and I felt a surge of satisfaction. Even if Jakob didn't shoot the man, which I knew he wouldn't, it was amusing to see him so blanched and terrified for his life.

Jakob smirked and then turned back to the lieutenant, lowering his pistol. "Can I shoot these two to prove my loyalty?" He asked, aiming the gun on the first officer this time, who flinched and stepped backwards, then sideways, paling further when the gun followed his movements.

Another barking laugh ripped from the lieutenant's mouth, but this time it didn't hold as much amusement as the last two times. This time I could hear the seriousness in his voice when he told him to put the gun down. "You know that isn't what I mean." He stated.

"Can I shoot them anyway?" He taunted, still being unconcerned with his speech.

The lieutenant's face turned dangerously dark, but he did nothing more than to clarify what he'd meant. "It's not them I want you to shoot, it's her."

I'd expected as much, and from the way Jakob's expression didn't change, so had he. It was obvious what the lieutenant had meant, and I found myself surprisingly grateful. They hadn't asked him to do anything that would cause me pain. It would be instant and then over with. I wouldn't have to suffer at all.

I lifted my eyes to Jakob's and tried to assure him that it was okay. I could see in his eyes that despite his placid expression, he was forcing himself not to shoot anyone that would cause him grief. I half expected him to turn the gun on the lieutenant himself. He didn't, though, much to my relief.

Now I just needed him to stick to his promise.

"You two, pick her up and hold her still."

In an instant I was being hoisted up by each arm, none to gently at that, and the two officers held me immobile, whilst trying to stay as far away as possible so they wouldn't be covered in blood when Jakob blew my brains out.

"In your own time, Officer Eichel." The lieutenant told him coldly, back to being all business. This was Jakob's moment of truth and if he failed, then he'd end up suffering the same inevitable fate as me.

Jakob looked at the gun, then back at me. With two shaky hands holding it, he lifted it so the aim was trained on the middle of my forehead. That way, it would give me an instant death. Jakob and I both knew that.

In the moment he'd turned the gun on me, his act of calmness had evaporated and he was giving away just how much he didn't want to do this.

He looked me dead in the face, but made no move to pull the trigger, instead, he was gazing at me in horror. He was telling me in his expression his views on what he thought of the promise he'd made to me earlier.

"Do it." I whispered, pleading with him with my eyes.

And he did it.

The hold on his gun became steadier and he looked back at me more resolutely.

Keeping the aim pointing at my forehead, without margin for error, he pulled the trigger and the shot rang out around the room.

EEK! How about that for a cliffhanger! Only one chapter and an epilogue left now! :D Though I'd let you know ;D

Thanks for votes and comments, hope this was okay :D

Chapter Sixteen

This is not the last chapter! Just to let you know before you read.

Chapter Sixteen…

I expected my death to be sudden, a shattering impact and then nothing, but it was much the opposite.

Instead of an abrupt blinding pain, all I felt was a graze along the side of my head where the bullet had skimmed my hairline and the sound of the bullet smashing into the wall behind me and then thudding to the floor. Although the gash was painful, and I could feel the blood dribbling down into my ear where it had tore shallowly at the skin, I was too overwhelmed by the fact I was still alive to pay any attention to it.

When I glanced back up at Jakob, my eyes wide with misunderstanding, his gun was pointing in completely the other direction where he'd swerved it at the last second. When he caught my gaze, he threw the gun to the side. "I can't do it." He finally decided.

I shook my head. "What are you doing?" I cried, forgetting myself for a moment. "Pick up the gun and shoot me Jakob."

I never thought I'd hear those words coming out of my mouth, but I didn't see the point in wanting to take them back once they'd slipped out. Maybe it would convince him that he'd done the wrong thing.

The lieutenant snorted. "Jakob, now, is it?" He inquired, sneering. "Well, aren't you going to do as the girl says? She clearly wants to die."

Jakob sent him a foul look, having accepted once and for all that his life was over now and not bothering to hold his tongue or attitude around the man anymore. Then, he turned and gave me a more tender look. "I'm not going to shoot you Viktória."

I sighed. "But you promised." I complained.

"Well then I lied."

He said it so blatantly that I felt like I should have got incredibly mad at him; yell that he couldn't just break promises like that. But, the fact he broke his promise so he didn't have to kill me, made it slightly more forgivable.

"Well, this is cute and all." The lieutenant interrupted our non-verbal communicating with his sarcastic comment. "But I'm guessing you know what that means, Officer Eichel?"

Jakob shrugged. "I can guess." He put forward.

The lieutenant adopted a satisfied look. "Oh, but I don't think you can." He taunted. "I'm not going to give you a simple death like you want! Oh no. I'm going to gas you, like the common Jew you've associated yourself with."

Jakob nodded. "I probably could have guessed that, to be honest." He remarked, ruining the lieutenant's placid look for a split second as he shot a venomous look at Jakob.

Then, it was back and his features were composed, complete with the natural arrogance that came with them. "And," He added cheerfully. "You get to work for a whole day as a Jew as well!"

Jakob didn't even flinch. "Okay." He agreed.

"It should be worse, but I like you." He admitted. "You have balls, I'll give you that much. I'm even going to let you die with your whore."

"She's not my whore." Jakob hissed harshly, not doing any favours for himself if he wanted to keep this 'presidential treatment' the lieutenant had so kindly bestowed upon him.

The lieutenant shrugged. "Same difference though." He waved Jakob off. "You'll still die with her."

I was still too amazed to really comprehend what was happening at the moment and I just stood there with my mouth hanging open unattractively. Jakob had given up his life. I couldn't say that it was for me, because well, it was more for his conscience than anything else. He didn't want to live with the guilt and I could understand that.

As long as he was the one who made the decision, I couldn't bring myself to feel guilty about it. It was his choice, after all, and I'd done I could so save his life.

And if Jakob had to die, then I was selfish enough to be glad it was with me.

A sudden wave in my direction from the lieutenant made me stiffen. I was about to see what would be happening to me before the gas chambers awaited. "You can let her go." He told the two officers who were still grasping my arms.

It was only when they let go that I realised how much I'd been relying on their support and I stumbled forward under my sudden weight. Jakob was instantly there to catch me and put me back on my feet again.

The second of the two officers, the tall thin one, jeered at him. "How can you become smitten with a fucking Jew?" He asked, disgusted. "Don't we even get to rape her once? Once each?"

I felt the hold Jakob still had on my arm become more possessive and I could guess his other fist was clenched. The lieutenant shrugged nonchalantly and I felt my heart drop in my chest. He didn't care about what happened to me, of course he didn't. He'd already thought he was being generous to Jakob, but he had no such inclinations when it came to me. "If you can get past Eichel without taking your guns out, then feel free."

I breathed a sigh of relief out when both the older men glanced at Jakob, who was well equipped with both youth and muscle. They shook their heads after checking with each other. "I think we'll go and find someone less protected." The first decided.

"Well then," the lieutenant turned back to Jakob. "We'd better get you some accommodation sorted out."

"I could just stay in my room and then get someone to wake me up when I need to work." He proposed hopefully, already knowing that he was going to get shot down before he'd said it.

The lieutenant snorted, an unattractive sound that reverberated off the room's walls. "Good try Eichel." He applauded, though his tone was not nearly as friendly as his words suggested. "But no, if you're going to get the full Jewish experience, then you at least have to stay in one of the huts, where the roofs are falling down and the cold seeps in through your little sheets that they dare to call a blanket."

He said it with such mocking that I felt my teeth clench. They knew exactly what kind of conditions we endured day after day, night after night, but it made no difference to them. We were a joke to them - a source of entertainment. How people could get enjoyment from other people's suffering was beyond me, but after my now first hand experiences, I saw that all of them relied on it.

The dead officer had summed it up perfectly for everybody here. "You've got to find pleasure where you can." He'd said. And all there was here to take pleasure in was our suffering. So that's what people did. It was a really sadistic way of life, but soon enough, I could see why everyone got used to it. I was shocked Jakob was still as generous and loving as he was. There wasn't a lot of reason to be any better, it was easier to just go along with it, so that's what everyone did.

They were all gullible and weak.

If enough of them stood up for us, then the establishment would be destroyed without trouble, but they'd gotten to used to the routine now, the effortlessness of shooting people, raping young girls who couldn't stop you even though they want to. If they bothered to rebel, then they'd never have life as easy again.

They were more bothered about themselves than the torture we were being put through.

"But," the lieutenant drew me out of my psychological analysis with his smarmy voice, full with false friendliness. "I will let you spend your last night with your missus, since I'm sure they'll be some spare beds in your shack by now, from where the roommates have perished." He gestured at me. "You can lie and freeze together." He feigned cheeriness, a sneering smile on his face as he enjoyed abusing his power over Jakob. "I would have said sleep, but I wouldn't want to imply anything."

I forced my cheeks to stay pale, so that I wouldn't give up the stony faced mask I was currently wearing. This omnipotent man wouldn't get the privilege of seeing me blush. There were some things even he couldn't control.

"I'll let these two lovely fellows escort you back to your hut, but," he turned to them then, narrowed eyes and a thin mouth instantly replacing the sarcastic grin he'd previously been wearing. "You hurt either of them and you'll be strung up whilst I chop off your cocks and shove them in your mouth."

Both their faces paled and I knew they wouldn't dare to defy the man addressing them. They were far too puny and scared to do that. It was the precise reason the lieutenant had 'taken' to Jakob, clearly despised the two officers who had brought Jakob to him. In the face of death, Jakob hadn't backed down and begged for his life, like these too weaklings no doubt would have done.

Jakob had certainly changed since the first time I'd met him.

All was silent, until the lieutenant let out an aggravated sigh and the two soldiers jumped nearly a foot into the air. Considering they'd been man-handling me mere minutes ago, fondling my most sensitive areas, the fact they were now hopping about like scared children afraid of being scolded, was quite comical, although I couldn't bring myself to even crack a smile at them due to the dire situation.

"Well, are you going to just stand there, or do what I told you?" He barked, obviously enjoying the fact he had them wrapped around his little finger, but showing how quick he was to anger as well. The mush of German expletives he mumbled under his breath wasn't faked.

They were instantly opening the door, having sprung to attention and carried out his orders within a split second. "Of course, sir." They chorused like sheep.

"I'll be keeping an eye on the two of you." He warned, although it didn't sound like a threat, more of an event he was going to enjoy attending. "It'll be interesting to see how you behave with the knowledge you'll be dying that evening."

With that, he waved a hand to dismiss us and I felt Jakob link his arm through mine as he steered me out of the room as quickly as he could. We were instantly tailed, but the knowledge we couldn't be hurt by them made me feel much safer.

Knowing that their presence wasn't particularly needed, they settled to follow as far behind as they could get, where they could make their japes privately and not risk us tattling on them to the lieutenant if we should be that way inclined.

"I'm sorry I didn't just do it." Jakob told me seriously as soon as we were out of earshot. "I know I broke my promise, and the lieutenant, he could have done some horrible stuff to you." He shuddered and I placed a comforting hand and his arm, which was still linked through mine.

"It's fine." I assured him gently. "I'm glad you didn't kill me." I admitted. "But I wish you could have lived."

I felt my eyes cloud with tears, but once again I held them back. I wouldn't let Jakob see just how upset I was, otherwise he might feel even worse. It was his decision in the end, and if his life wasn't that important to him, then it wasn't for me to say whether he should keep it or not.

Jakob smiled softly. "I wouldn't have lived happily." He assured me. "So I'd rather die with you."

The bluntness of the way he was saying it still didn't fail to shock me, though I'd said it just as readily. I. Was. Going. To Die. Simple as that.

Yet, it still didn't quite seem real to me.

I was walking through the buildings still, which was strange, but soon I'd been back into the night, surrounded by the rundown huts and shacks. I wouldn't be shackled, or confined in any way that was worse than the obvious, but then I'd be losing my life in less than twenty four hours.

I just expected the lead up to my death to be different somehow.

At least being shot was more dramatic, this way seemed far to peaceful. It was too arranged. I could see now why the lieutenant had been interested to see how this played out. The predetermined time of my death was going to be constantly playing on my mind, and I knew that. It was going to rule every action that I made, make me cautious of doing things I'd regret and then not get the chance to put right.

I tried to put it from my thoughts though, as hard as that was, and concentrated on just getting back to the hut. Then, I could say what I really wanted without the potentially prying ears of the two frightened conformists listening in and spreading around to whoever would be willing to hear.

It didn't take us long, and I was pleased to see that there was still no signs of sun in the sky. It was pitch black and although the past few hours had seemed like a lifetime, they hadn't really been that long at all. I still had the rest of the night and day before I would be walking the Earth no longer.

There was still time to get things sorted.

"Have fun in your new accommodation." The first officer sneered, no longer so afraid that he wouldn't open his mouth against Jakob any longer. There was no one's threats bearing down on him from here. "I'm sure you'll be nice and freezing."

Jakob gave him a much harsher look in return and I knew that there was pure and unrefined anger in him. It was startling so see how enraged he'd become and if I hadn't known him better, I would have flinched away from him. "I will," he assured them, his voice scathing. "You know why? Because I'm not living a lie, where I abuse young girls and force them into my bed, thinking that I'm doing them a favour because I'm a sad and pathetic old man. I'm dying for a cause, you're just going along with whatever they brainwash you to believe, because you're weak and scared. You'll die on the end of a rope when the British and French come to shut this abomination of a place down. And if you think I'm wrong, then you're just kidding yourself."

The man he'd insulted let out a growl of unadulterated fury. "Don't you dare talk to me like that." He hissed, advancing on Jakob, made fearless by anger. "Who do you think you are? What right do you have to insult me?"

"The rights of a dead man." Jakob responded seriously. His voice considerably calmer than it had been when he'd first started his rant.

With renewed resentment, the stout, round soldier lunged at Jakob, his fist raised as he planned to sent a blow to Jakob's head. "You can be dead a hell of a lot quicker if I have anything to do about it."

I had instantly relinquished Jakob's hold on my arm and stepped sideways, as far away from the fray as possible without causing concern. Jakob caught the man's fist and twisted, so that he was forced to his knees, hopeless against the strength Jakob had behind his grip. "And if you even consider that, then you'll be the eunuch giving himself a suck."

The threat obviously weighed heavily on the both of them, because the second officer hadn't even made a move to defend his colleague when Jakob had brought him to his knees. He hadn't even sent a glance my way when he moved. He was obviously more concerned about his own life than anyone else's - much like everyone else around here.

"I think we'll go now." The first officer spat out through his shame and rage, his face a bright crimson compared to the paleness it had adopted in the lieutenants office.

"That's what I thought." Jakob remarked. "Now, you can go back to your normal shallow lives, raping teenagers and abusing innocent people."

With that, he opened the door to our hut and didn't look back as he retook my arm and guided me in, breaking away my eye contact with the two men, who were rapidly retreating, looking just as frightened as they had when the lieutenant looked at them the wrong way. Jakob muttered something unintelligible, but clearly negative, about them in German, shaking his head as we walked silently over to my bunk bed, not wanting to disturb anyone.

When we got to it, Jakob knowing which one it was from the many times he had 'inspected' my bunk on his daily rounds, I noticed once again that the bottom bunk was empty. The lieutenant's words rang back to me and I realised that she must be one of the perished ones he was talking about. She'd died.

But, to avoid risking waking people up, I sat down on it anyway, trying not to think that by tomorrow there would be no one sleeping in my bed either. Jakob took a seat next to me and I rested my head on his shoulder.

Neither of us spoke, because neither of us knew what to say. What was there to say right now? I'm sorry we're going to die? It wasn't really a conversation starter, it was just a fact. What was the point in ruining what seemed like a normal moment with all that factual talk? I'd rather be happy in Jakob's company, with his arm, which had wrapped itself securely around my waist, giving me the heat I'd been without all the other nights I'd been here.

"You should go to sleep." He whispered softly, stroking my hair with his free hand. "You've been awake all day and all night."

Despite the fact I could feel my eyes drooping, I still managed to shake my head. "No." I told him seriously. "I can't go to sleep, I want to spend all the time I have left with you."

He smiled and pressed a gentle kiss to my forehead. "I really am sorry." He told me, his voice ringing with both sincerity and sadness. "You'd still be alive tomorrow if I'd just left you alone in the first place."

I decided to rearrange our positions before I answered, so that we were laid down on the bed, side by side and almost falling over the edge with the miniscule sizes of the bunks. He still wrapped both arms around me, though, and I snuggled into him, feeling more secure than I had in a long time.

"That's not true." I assured him, like I had many times before that having him in my life wasn't something I'd ever take back. "If you hadn't helped me in the first place, then I'd have either died of starvation by now, or ended up like Stephánia, raped every night just to keep enough food in my belly to live." I reminded him. "And if you hadn't helped earlier, then I'd have ended up being raped regardless. I'd rather die now, with all my virtues still intact, than later when half the soldiers in the place have realised I'm on offer."

I felt him wince, so I just grasped his hand and assured him with my body language that I was grateful for everything I'd done for him.

"And most of all, if you'd never interfered in the first place, I'd never have loved you. And that's not something I could ever take back."

He kissed me so fiercely then I thought I was imagining things. With us, it had always been soft pecks and tender embraces, that showed the gentleness in the both of us. I think Jakob had always done that to prove he wasn't the same tough, careless monster that lived inside the other men, but that he was kind and honest in his intentions.

This, this was completely different, though.

This was passionate and heated and I soon found that my breath had disappeared. I pushed myself tighter against him and waited until I would have suffocated myself before I brought myself to pull away.

"I love you Viktória." Jakob whispered desperately. "I love you so fucking much."

I bit my lip and this time, when the tears invaded my vision, I didn't try to stop them. "I love you too." I replied, my voice quivering and my hands shaking as they rested gently on his chest. "I wish this could have been different."

"Me too."

I felt him wipe the tears that had trailed down my face with the pad of this thumb, but his touch was gentle this time and when I glanced back at his face, I saw the wet trails gleaming down his own cheeks. I'd never expected him to cry, but I understood it nevertheless. He'd been afraid to die the last time, that couldn't have just disappeared. He was sacrificing a lot for his conscience this time as well.

We gave each other teary smiles, both hit with the realisation that this would be the last night we'd ever see.

*** *** *** *** *** *** *** *** *** *** *** *** *** ***

I knew even when I'd said it that I'd drift off, but I tried to stay awake for as long as possible. I talked to Jakob about anything and everything. We'd share kisses, tell each other the things we'd wished as children we could have done - all the things that had been lost to us the moment we entered this place.

Then, so much quicker than it should have been, the morning was upon us.

Light streamed through the several holes in the roof and walls, but not enough to blind us, due to how early they woke us up every morning, but when the doors banged open and the two soldiers came bursting in, I was still forced to squint my eyes.

Everyone was up in a flurry, knowing the routine by now, and nobody's eyes even strayed to the two of us, even though Jakob was still dressed in his officer's uniform.

No one apart from the soldier's, anyway. "Eichel?" One of them demanded, incredulously. He was quite young as well, which I was surprised about; most of them seemed at least in their forties; but he was only about five years older than Jakob. "What are you doing bruder?"

I recognised the word for brother, and was almost surprised. I'd never considered the fact that Jakob might have friends within the staff here. I'd always just assumed he hated them all, like I did. But, this officer seemed rather friendly towards him, a lot better than the other officers anyway, who all held a large amount of resentment from what I'd picked up on.

"Dying happy." Was Jakob's response, as casual as if he'd been saying he was taking a piss. He was also completely serious, though.

I slapped his arm, hard. "Don't say it like that!" I scolded, grimacing.

He raised an eyebrow at me. "Would you want me to die sad, Viktória?" He inquired.

"Well, no, but I still wish you would say it so...so easily! I didn't want you to die."

"And I didn't want to shoot you." He declared, smiling gently at me, and then standing up, offering me a hand to pull me up, knowing that even if he was on good terms with this officer, that we wouldn't be allowed to dawdle anymore than the rest of them.

The soldier had walked over to Jakob by the time we were on our feet and was regarding Jakob with a genuinely puzzled expression. "I'll admit that I'm lost." He said seriously, letting his eyes scan over me with the same curious scrutiny, but not the leering expression everyone else seemed to greet me with. There was no malicious intent in there.

Jakob sighed, a heavy sound that gave away just how much he wasn't looking forward to the evening's events. He quickly scanned over shooting the man and then the main events in the lieutenant's room. "So, I die tonight." He finally finished. "And unfortunately, I take her with me."

He wrapped an arm around my waist in the most public display of affection I'd ever had. We had the entire hut's attention now as well, since there was no one giving them orders anymore.

"You'll be missed," the young soldier said, honesty shining through in his tone. "I'm sorry you have to go this way, but you always knew you'd be a sucker for someone in the end, didn't you? You're too soft."

Jakob smirked. "And you'll die a lonely old man." Jakob responded, his voice teasing rather than the enraged threat he'd given the stout officer earlier tonight. "But either way, I'm not complaining. I should have died the first time I was given the option."

The young officer shook his head, exasperated. "I never knew you were so negative Jakob." He remarked. "But, I guess we'd better get you working. I'll not be in the good books if I let you slack off."

A quick, sharp nod of the head from Jakob made the other officer, who hadn't said anything whilst we'd been in here, settling to just listen and keep his opinions to himself, give the order to get moving out and hurried them along. It seemed that even though he was clearly not a 'soldier' anymore, he still had some sort of authority and the officer had responded to his gesture immediately. The inmates followed his commands instantaneously and I instantly recognised the similarities between their reactions to the ones of the two soldiers who'd been with us most of the night.

The young officer stayed behind to talk to Jakob though as everyone else filed out. He turned to me as we followed them out. "I'm Matthäus, by the way," he told me with a genuine smile, before picking up my hand and kissing it softly. "It is a shame we didn't get the chance to know each other better, schatz." I recognised the word for sweetheart, because Jakob had called me it several times.

I flushed whilst Jakob rolled his eyes. "Keep your hands off her Matthäus." He warned, seriously. "If I'm dying for her, then you'd better find someone else to give your affections to."

Matthäus smiled, but I knew he wasn't going to disrespect Jakob like that. He seemed like a nice man. "I wouldn't dream of touching her." Then, he paused. "Well, I might dream of it, she is sehr schön. I can see why you went for her."

Jakob shook his head in part amusement and part despair. "Very beautiful." He whispered gently in my ear when he saw my confused look. I blushed deeper and Jakob sighed. "You're such a sweet talker Matty." He complained. "But you're right. She is sehr schön." Jakob gave me a quick peck on the lips before we braved the real word beyond the hut.

Jakob and I separated once we had left the shack and we were instantly surrounded by the hustle of moving bodies hurrying to work and follow commands. "Good luck." Matthäus told the both of us; but mainly Jakob. "I really am sorry to see you go bruder."

Jakob smiled sadly. "Me too bruder, me too. You've been a good friend."

They conversed quickly with some short German phrases and small, sad laughs escaped their mouths before they shared a quick hug and broke apart. Matthäus kissed my hand again and this time I managed to control my red cheeks. "Take care of him." He told me seriously. "He deserves that. He's a good man."

I felt the tears brim and one escaped, slipping down my face. I'd only just met this man and yet I already felt like I would trust him if it came down to it. "I promise." I whispered. "I love him just as much as you do."

Matthäus grinned. "That's all I needed to here." He assured me. "I wish he'd told me about you earlier schatz. I know we could have been great friends."

I smiled faintly. "I'm sure." I agreed. "It's good to have met you, Matthäus."

We shared a smile, but then everyone was moving rapidly and we knew we had to go too. Jakob and Matthäus shared another quick brotherly hug and then we had been swept along by the rest of the crowd.

Although everyone generally avoided us, because of Jakob's uniform, we couldn't just be left here once everyone else was gone. Jakob had to play the part of any other inmate, which involved standing in the queues and obeying the orders.

I just hoped we could get through the day doing that, before the chambers started calling, because I still needed to speak to Stephánia.

Yes, there was only meant to be one more chapter for this, but I couldn't fit it all in one and it would have taken me forever to upload, so now there's only one chapter and an epilogue left. So, 18 chapters all together!

Hope this was okay, tell me what you're thinking, and don't ask about Matthaus, spur of the moment addition, I felt that Jakob should at least have someone to miss him!

Thanks for votes and comments, hope you enjoy this!

Chapter Seventeen

C hapter Seventeen...

It was safe to say that Jakob had attracted all the attention throughout the day. Officers had turned their heads to stare in both amazement and disgust to see a uniformed officer dismantling glasses like a common Jew.

And the inmates had been no different. They had watched with clear curiosity and incredulity as Jakob worked, didn't complain once and followed all the orders he was given, whilst ignoring the jeers and insults from the officers who now looked down on him.

We were incredibly lucky that Matthäus had been the one handing out rations when it got to that time, because, knowing it was our last day, he gave us bigger share of the food than Jakob had ever given me. It was accompanied with a sad smile, accepting the fact it would be the last one we'd see from him.

When the day was over, I'd managed to gash my hands to even more of an extreme than even the first time I'd dismantled the spectacles. My mind had been elsewhere the entire time: thinking over what was going to happen tonight, thinking over what could never happen because of tonight and thinking over how I was going to break this to Stephánia.

That was the hardest. Stephánia had confessed everything to me. She'd told me about her rape, she'd spoke about the worst experience in her entire life to me, and then I would be gone, and she would be alone. I was the only thing she had left here, the only person she could trust. When I was gone, not even Jakob would be here to look out for her.

I locked eyes with him then, from at the side of me where he was walking a respectable distance away. We didn't want to push anyone's buttons even walking back to the hut, so had chosen not to give people any more of a reason to single us out. It had been bad enough already, but at least no one had associated me with Jakob, so I'd been left out of all the japes and luckily received no attention.

When we got to the shack, we instantly retreated to my bunk, with the two empty beds, and sat down, unsure of what we should do now. "Will they just come for us?" I asked, not wanting to think about it, but knowing I had to be aware if I wanted to find Stephánia in time.

Jakob nodded. "I should have thought so, but I'm just as in the dark as you." He admitted. "We should have time to visit Stephánia, though." He assured me, already having predicted my line of thought.

"Good," I murmured, dreading that meeting. What was I going to say? Stephánia would be devastated, and even though I knew there was nothing I could do about it, that it was out of my control, I'd still feel insanely guilty - I already did.

Jakob shot me a sympathetic look and I knew he had once again read my thoughts. He placed a comforting hand on my arm, rubbing a soothing circle into it as I tried to collect the snippets of things I'd realised I wanted to say today. "She'll be fine without you." He said gently.

"She wasn't fine with me." I pointed out bitterly. "I didn't do anything that stopped her abuse, why should she even be bothered that I'm going to die in the first place?"

I knew it wasn't the truth, but the sudden rush of helplessness that consumed me made me blurt the things that nagged at the back of my mind. I'd done nothing for Stephánia whilst I'd been here, I'd lied to her about her family, about the girl who carried the dead bodies, about Jakob. She shouldn't trust me and she shouldn't miss me when I was gone.

She still would, though.

I rested my head on Jakob's shoulder momentarily, whilst he tried his best to convince me that I was spouting out rubbish in the heat of the moment. The only problem was, that when he tried to tell me that Stephánia would be lost about me, that made the guilt set back in and I felt even worse.

There was no easy solution to this, nothing that a few cheery words could solve, and either way, I would be gone soon enough.

I stood up suddenly, with renewed determination. "Come on, we need to go and find her." I said resolutely. I should get this over and done with, before it became too late. The men in charge weren't going to be forever coming to collect us. They wouldn't care about who I was leaving behind; or Jakob, for that matter.

Jakob stood up behind me and followed as I walked to the door, my face set in stone, my mouth a flat line filled with resolve and the sadness I was trying to conceal.

Only, the door opened just as I'd outstretched my arm to do the same thing. In a panic, thinking it was the officers coming to fetch us already, I backed into Jakob, who wrapped a protective arm around my waist immediately.

The face that appeared in the newly revealed gap was not a foe, though, and Stephánia's worried expression was what filled it instead. "Viktória?" She asked, taking in my position and allowing her appearance to become even more wary. "What's happened? Why is he here? Why do you look so scared?"

I tried to rearrange my face and wipe away the fearful look I'd unknowingly plastered onto it. I also pealed myself away from Jakob, trying to ignore the stares that all the remaining girls in the hut had given us. Despite having seen Jakob this morning, apparently the novelty hadn't worn off, and we were still earning the inquisitive gazes, though at least everyone here was too nervous to speak to us.

"Lets just sit down." I told Stephánia distractedly, walking towards my bunk and sitting down, patting the seat next to me. Jakob chose to stand, so as not to crowd the already overloaded bunk.

She glanced at me expectantly and it was only now that I realised all words had failed me. For all the planning I'd done throughout the day, when the time had come, I was speechless. Everything was garbled in my mind and I could feel Stephánia heavy gaze on me, waiting for some clue as to what was happening.

"Viktória, what's wrong?" Stephánia pressed, her voice becoming more urgent. "What have you done?"

I felt the tears accumulating as I met her frantic gaze. "I'm going to die." I whispered, biting my lip as a drop of water slipped down my cheek unscathed.

Stephánia, who was staring at me with wide eyes, let out a sudden bark of humourless laughter, filled with a biting stroke of madness. "Isn't everyone?" She inquired darkly. "When are you going to die, Viktória?"

"Tonight." I declared nervously, hoping I didn't inspire any more erratic behaviour from her. This was the first time I'd ever see her be so dark and negative - she was normally the one inspiring goodness in people. It told me what I'd known all along, that losing me would push her over the edge. She was letting that show with her cruel words and sour laughter.

Then, in a split second, she'd burst into inconsolable tears. I pulled her into a tight hug in an attempt to calm her down, but the sobs continued to rack through her body and I knew that my attempts were futile.

I found the tears running in irregular streams down my own cheeks as well, but I refused to let myself break down in the same way. I wasn't going to be that weak in the face of my death.

"You can't leave me Viktória, not like this." She blubbered, sniffling loudly and shaking with horror in my arms. She pulled back away from my grasp and stared at me with an empty gaze. "What am I supposed to do when your gone? They'll be no one. I'll be alone with rapists and murderers. How am I supposed to live like that? Can't I die with you?"

I shook my head softly, completely out of my depth when it came to convincing emotionally unstable best friends to keep living. "You just have to stay strong Stephánia." I told her soothingly. "It'll all be over soon." I assured her. "You'll forget I even existed soon."

She grasped my hands tightly with her own. "No I won't." She cried quietly, regarding me with wide and terrified eyes that gave the same appearance of madness that her laugh had evoked. "I won't. I'll always remember you, but I can't do it by myself."

I forced out a watery smile. "You can do it by yourself. You're a strong person Stephánia, and it won't be forever. There are other people here, people you can trust, I'm sure."

She suddenly scowled. "I don't trust Jakob," she replied bitterly. "I don't care how much you love him."

My face darkened and I couldn't help my attempt at a pleasant expression slipping from my features and a bleak grimace replaced it. "Jakob's going to die too." I monotoned, unwilling to show just how much that meant to me whilst Stephánia disregarded any support he would have given her.

Her face rearranged in shock and she glanced at me sympathetically. "I'm sorry, Viktória, ,I didn't realise-"

I cut her off with a sharp shake of the head and a flat look. "You don't care, Stephánia, I know you don't, but I do. Jakob could have lived, if he'd shot me, but he didn't. Does that prove to you that he's different?" I told her virulently, unable to keep the coldness from my voice. "The fact he gave up his life means nothing to you, does it? Still just a German soldier in your eyes."

This was exactly what I'd meant when I'd realised that I would say things I couldn't take back. I would take that back in an instant if I could, having seen the look on Stephánia's face. I couldn't help it, though. I was overwhelmed by everything and my emotions were all over the place, I was going to die tonight, I was allowed to be extravagant in everything I said and did.

I didn't want to upset Stephánia with my all over the place emotions though.

She glanced at me with wide eyes and I could see the tears building up in them again. I flushed in shame at my unnecessary snappiness. "I'm sorry, Stephánia, I'm sorry, I didn't mean it, I'm just upset and I-"

She cut me off. "No," She interrupted, grasping my hands tighter. "I'm sorry." She apologised. "I'm sorry I never could accept him for you. I'm sorry you're going to die, but I'm going to do live for you, I'll do it Viktória, I'll live for you."

He was crying again and so was I, but both for very different reasons. I was crying for the happiness that Stephánia would at least try to be okay. She was crying because I was going to die.

It was the opposite of how it should have been, really, but that didn't matter. I was just glad she was going to try. Even if it didn't succeed and she ended up losing her life through her own fault, I could say I'd tried my hardest and that she had too. The sincerity rang clear in her expression and voice, and I knew that Stephánia meant it when she said she'd live for as long as she could bare it.

Not that I'd ever know the consequences from beyond the grave.

We were suddenly in another tight hug and we clung to each other desperately with the realisation that this would be the last time we could embrace in such a way. "I love you Viktória." She whispered gently, her words choked and hoarse with emotion.

"I love you too Stephánia." I replied, feeling the tears wash faster down my face. Stephánia had become more like the sister that I'd never had in this short space of time than the friend she'd been back in Ajka. She was the person, other than Jakob, that I really didn't want to leave behind.

That was when I heard the door kicked in forcefully. I knew what was happening before I turned my head to watch the lieutenant stalking his way towards us purposefully. "My newest friends!" He announced, grinning with false friendliness. Then, his face turned down into a pout. "It is a shame that it's time to die."

I pulled away from Stephánia and stood up next to Jakob. Stephánia cried harder and I placed a gentle hand on her shoulder. "See you on the other side." I said gently, finally putting a plug in my tears and managing to keep a straight face now I was in the presence of the monster who was putting us to our deaths.

Stephánia didn't have any of the same concerns, however, and she burst into another round of grief-stricken sobs. "I'll miss you Viktória." She choked out through her bawling, giving me one last watery smile before the lieutenant talked again and my attention was returned to him.

"Lets go, chop chop." He clapped his hands in aggravation, though his voice was still far too cheery for the dire situation. "We don't want to keep the gas men waiting."

The three soldiers who he'd brought with him were of an unknown identity to me and they made a move to come and grab us, but the lieutenant shook his head and they immediately backed down. "They'll come on their own." He told the tallest man, a smug smile on his wrinkling face. "What would be the point in dying an even more demeaning death?"

He was right, Jakob and I both knew it. There was no point in fighting now, it would just mean being dragged through the yards by soldiers, an even more humiliating event. If we came calmly, we'd at least get to walk with each other, bask in our last minutes of one another's presence.

I walked out of the hut with as much dignity as I could, Jakob as close beside me as he could get, and I glanced back at Stephánia once, to meet her fraught eyes and the sheer desperation in his expression.

I couldn't even bring myself to give her a smile, but I knew that my gaze was conveying all that I couldn't say. After a few mere seconds, I returned my stare back to the direction I was going, and I didn't look back. There was nothing there I could change, and reminiscing on it now would only make me feel more guilty.

I just needed to keep my thoughts on the here and now.

When we were out of the building, the lieutenant sidled up beside me, much to my shock. I thought he'd be only interesting in talking to Jakob, but I also realised that maybe he was only here to leer at me.

He didn't, though, and chose to sneer instead. "That was very emotional back there." He commented nonchalantly. "Such a poor girl. It almost makes me want to keep you alive."

"No it doesn't." I deadpanned, grimacing.

He smirked. "Ah, you're right, but I was trying to be nice."

"No you weren't."

Instead of showing any signs of irritation, though, the lieutenant's smile widened. "Ah, and you're right again!" He declared. "It is a shame you doubt my intentions' integrity. You should be grateful I let you last this long. The day's events have been frightfully boring and I was tempted to just shoot you in the middle of everyone, to see how that would make everything play out, but alas, I'm not that heartless. I did promise you the chambers after all."

I snorted, only now realising how Jakob had been so brave last night. This was what he'd felt, the courage that came with your inevitable doom. There was nothing he could do to hurt me now, so I might as well give him the satisfaction of hearing what was really going on inside my head, to know the real person he was sending to the grave.

"Why, how generous of you." I stated, my voice thick with bitter sarcasm.

The lieutenant grinned arrogantly. "I knew you'd appreciate it." He returned, his voice also containing the same amount of sarcasm as my own. He turned to Jakob then, who was gritting his teeth in anger and holding his tongue against some snappy remark. "And how have you found the day Off-oh wait, I can't really call you an officer any more, can I Eichel?"

"You say it as though I appreciated the title in the first place. You know I only picked it over torture and death, since you were the one threatening me, after all."

The lieutenant smirked maliciously. "And haven't you changed from the snivelling boy I watched as I shot your father in front of you? I could even consider you a man now."

Jakob had never told me he watched his father die, and he certainly hadn't said that the lieutenant had been the one to shoot him, but I guessed there was some things that didn't want, or need, saying aloud.

When I glanced at him now, the look on his face conveyed the thunder he was managing to control. "And you're still exactly the same bastard that I remember."

The lieutenant was unfazed and we both knew that was because he had nothing to fear. Jakob and I were as good as dead now; he just had the audacity to be entertained with us and our now fearless remarks on the way there.

"So, how are you looking forward to your deaths, then? You appear to have had a rather normal day considering. Well, for this young lady, anyway. I doubt your work was exactly what you're used to Eichel." He remarked, the ever permanent smirk still plastered across his sneering lips.

Jakob didn't rise to the bait though, and I didn't miss the disappointment that flashed in the lieutenant's eyes at that. "I enjoyed my day perfectly well, thank you lieutenant." He replied formally. "May I return the courtesy and ask how you enjoyed yours? I often doubt that being a lonely old man is a particularly good career. Then again, torturing people for your pleasure kind of makes me understand why you chose this job."

This time, both Jakob and I got the satisfaction of seeing the lieutenant's expression darken. That had hit a nerve, no doubt about it, and the smirk changed allegiance quickly, occupying Jakob's usually kind mouth instead.

"You should watch your mouth, Eichel." The lieutenant warned seriously, the threat fitting right in with the cold glint in his eyes.

"Why?" Jakob inquired frankly. "What does a dead man have to fear?"

"You aren't dead yet." The lieutenant replied correctly. "There's still a lot that can go wrong for you." To prove his point, he grabbed me around the waist from where he was still stood beside me and placed the tip of his gun against my temple.

Jakob's face darkened, but he made no move to change the position I'd found myself in, knowing it would be futile. "Viktória's also dead, no matter what I do." He reminded the lieutenant.

I could hear the tension in Jakob's voice and I knew that he was bluffing, even if the lieutenant didn't. He cared, he just didn't want to give the abomination of a man before him even more ammo.

The lieutenant still wasn't put off by Jakob's blasé reaction though and smirked wider. "You're going to let me kill yet another one of your loved ones? And I thought you'd changed, I guess I was wrong."

He cocked the gun and I gulped. "Stop." Jakob stated, ripping me from the lieutenant's grasp and putting me on the other side of him, wrapping a protective arm around my waist. "Don't touch her, I'll shut up."

"Damn right you will." The lieutenant remarked darkly.

The rest of the journey was walked in silence. I could feel myself getting more tired the further we went. I'd slept no more than a wink last night and the chambers were even further away from my hut than I thought the camp extended.

My fatigue didn't stop me observing my surroundings, though. It was strange being anywhere other than in my shack and in the large building where I dismantled glasses and despite how much I hated both those places, the further we went, the more I wanted to go back.

It wasn't just the fact that I knew this walk led me to my death, though, the actual place was much grimmer than where I was used to staying, and that wasn't only because it was where people died; people including Jakob and I.

The buildings, if possible, got more derelict here; they were missing roofs and whole walls were subsiding. There was litter all around, which included the bones of men, women, children and, from the looks of the smallest ones, babies as well. I flinched when we walked particularly close to two skeletons, an extremely small one and a larger one. A mother and child. They weren't labelled, but it was obvious who they were.

Then, in a sudden transformation, the surroundings changed. There were no more falling down buildings, but solid structures which were even more modern than the soldier's buildings themselves.

They were just as grey and industrial looking, in rows upon rows into the distance, where I couldn't see the end of them. Each one had been built identically, they weren't very tall, but made up for that with length and width.

As we walked past one, I felt my face pale and Jakob's arm tightened around my waist, so that I could bury my face into his chest.

I could hear the screams of agony as thousands of people breathed in the poisonous gas. I couldn't pick out any individual voices, which was the worst thing. They were just a group of people that were dying. Nobody special, just a crowd of dead people who would come out so disfigured that no one would be able to tell them apart in the end anyway.

I tried to close my ears, but it didn't work. The screams still haunted my thoughts even after we'd walked so far past that I could even see the chamber any more.

Or at least I thought I couldn't, it was impossible to tell them apart.

The lieutenant came to sudden stop and I felt my heart rate increase in my chest. This was it. He'd stopped in front of a chamber identical to the rest, but somehow different as well.

This was the place we'd die at.

"Welcome to the gates of hell." The lieutenant announced, gesturing to the grey building with an extravagant movement of both arms.

I cringed into Jakob, hating how I was so afraid now it had gotten to the moment. I'd tried to resolve with myself that I'd take this like a man. I wouldn't whimper and shy away from the gases when they came to claim my life. I would inevitably scream in anguish, but not before it was impossible to hold it in.

"Open the door for the varmints." The lieutenant told the soldiers he'd asked to accompany him. Then he turned to us with that same smugness even more predominant on his features now. "Normally we'd make you strip off now, but I thought you might like to retain at least some dignity. I'm going to let you keep you garments." Then his eyes raked over me scornfully. "If you can even call those clothes."

A loud creak from the heavy iron door that concealed the entrance to the chamber startled me and in my already nervous state, I jumped and flinched. Jakob glanced at me, but I didn't meet his gaze. I didn't want him to see how scared I was.

The lieutenant once again fought to get our attention back onto him. "I can't say I'm going to miss either of you particularly, although Eichel, you would have made a great torturer one day, I'm sure. That really is a shame." He pouted again and I scowled shamelessly. Jakob could never torture someone, except maybe the monstrosity of a man that stood before us now. "So, in you get, and have some fun in there! You know it'll be the last chance you get."

He finished with his voice on a teasing note and watched with a grim satisfaction as we took tentative steps into the chamber.

It was pitch black due to the lack of windows and only the sliver of light from the door which was still open allowed me to see that the inside was completely bare. That was soon gone though and the darkness enveloped us, so that Jakob's arm around my waist was the only sense of my surroundings I had left.

"We need to get to the edge." He told me quickly. "That's where we'll last the longest."

I nodded and let him guide me to a wall, where we scooted along to a corner, which was where we stayed.

"I love you." I whispered, as I heard the gas holes being unscrewed from the roof.

I pretended that I could see Jakob smiling in the dark when he replied. "I love you too."

"I'm scared." I admitted, seeing no point in denying it now. "I don't want to die."

Jakob's arms enveloped me properly as I heard the gas being dispensed into the room. "I'm scared too and I don't want to die either." He repeated what I'd said and I started shaking, clinging to him desperately.

"Make love to me, Jakob." I begged him quietly, lifting my hands up to feel the features of his face.

I could feel his eyes on my face, even if I could see them. "We're about to die, Viktória." He reminded me seriously, as I felt the air around me become clammy.

I sighed. "I know. This is the last thing I can have that I really want. I want to lose my virtue to the man that I love."

Jakob gave me a gentle peck on the lips. "Are you sure?" He checked once more.

I nodded against his chest, so that I knew he could feel it, then dragged his lips back to mine once more, kissing him fiercely and with more determination than I'd ever felt before. I was going to do this and I was going to do it before the increasingly suffocating air stopped me.

He returned the gesture with equal fervour and I soon found myself breathless - and not from the choking gas that was spreading around me.

As the intensity of our kiss and exploration of each other's bodies got stronger, so did the gas and I knew that my breathlessness and the burning in my lungs was becoming the side effects of that rather than the heat I was feeling deep in the pit of my stomach.

"Do it." I told Jakob hoarsely. "Do it now."

He did.

After one more deep kiss, he began undoing his trousers and then lifting my hips to the correct position.

I took a deep breath as he tore through my maidenhead, but that breath was the final one I got.

That was when the burning started properly, when the pain became too much.

I cried out, but whether it was from ecstasy or agony, I wasn't sure.

And that's it! That's the end of the story :(

There's just the epilogue to come now!

So, I'd like to know exactly what you think of it. Do you think I rushed it? Do you think I wrote it badly? Seriously, other than the fact that they died, which has always been going to happen in the end, what was your opinion on it!

Thanks for all the votes and comments, they've been really inspiring and I'm so glad so many people thought I'd captured the time period well! Out of all my stories, this is the one I think is best written and the one I've enjoyed writing the most. It's certainly been the most interesting with the most stable plot.

So, I hope this was good, vote and comment please, and then await the epilogue, which will give a quick insight into Stephania's head!

Really thanks again and I hope this wasn't too disappointing!

And for once, I picked out the song especially, so... tell me if you think it fits with the chapter!

Epilogue

Epilogue:

Stephánia strolled through the graveyard, as she often did, her eyes sweeping over the various headstones, some shining in their newness and others crumpling in their dilapidation. She had known none of them personally, but still felt sorry for the many who had died at an unnecessarily young age.

When she reached the grave she had come to mourn at, she dropped to her knees before it. Caressing the letters that had been embellished into the hard stone, she let a tear slip from the corner of her eye. Viktória Horváth the letters read, the date of her memorable death next to it.

Stephánia let a small sob escape her chest. She missed Viktória dearly and still found it hard to accept her death, despite how long ago it had been. After six months she should have been able to get of Viktória's death, but somehow, it just kept coming back to haunt her. Viktória had been with her through everything and the thought that she wouldn't be able to help her with the upcoming trauma that was about to engulf her had brought tears to her eyes many times, just as it did now.

She looked further down the gravestone then, Jakob Eichel, the name was engraved beneath Viktória's. Stephánia didn't touch these letters, but she didn't dismiss them either. Despite knowing that Jakob had been partly responsible for Viktória's death, Stephánia had not been able to miss his name off. He had been everything to Viktória in the end and she deserved to be with him on the grave.

The speech Viktória had given when defending Jakob's intentions had been enough for Stephánia to fathom at least some admiration for the man and after all, they had died together. It only seemed right that their names were together, even if the actual bodies had never been recovered; or were just too disfigured in the end to be recognised.

As a habit that Stephánia had recently gained, she brushed her fingertips against her increasingly swelling stomach, once again wishing that Viktória could be here. She would have known what to do in this situation. She would have offered some comfort. She wouldn't have left Stephánia stranded with a baby on the way; no money or job to help support a family.

Stephánia grimaced at her belly then. She still hadn't quite gotten to terms with that part of her life.

Getting out of Auschwitz had been a blur. One day, she'd been underneath the grunting officer; the next she was being forced on a death march outside the camp, the furthest she'd been since arriving; then the day after that, she was under Soviet protection, being fed the first warm meal she'd tasted in months.

That had all been well and good, until the realisation of what had been planted inside her became evident. She was still traumatised enough by the abuse she'd suffered, but knowing she had a lasting piece of that currently inside her was almost enough to push her over the edge.

A gentle hand was placed on her shoulder then and Stephánia quickly remembered the reason she had made it in the end.

"It's okay, Stephy." Amália, Stephánia's younger sister assured her, in a voice that was a lot more grown up than Stephánia could ever remember it having been in Ajka. Even the way Amália used the nickname she'd always had for her wasn't in the same carefree way.

Mind you, she had her excuses. Amália had been the control twin of the experiments, she'd been given a clean room, good meals and left alone by any possible abusers. They monitored her to see if there was any change in her when they experimented on her twin Renáta.

She'd watched her sister Renáta have the most horrific things done to her, far too many appalling events for a child of twelve to witness. In the end, Renáta had been too disfigured and weak to join the death marches and Amália had watched Renáta's final breaths be taken as the officers gave her a clean death in the form of a bullet to the head.

But, in the Soviet camps, Stephánia and Amália had found one another again and at least gained some kind of positive outcome from the events which had followed their initial separation.

Another sob ripped unbidden from Stephánia's throat and she shook her head in response to her younger sister's statement. "I can't do it Amália." She whispered distraughtly. "I can't do this."

As if the fact she had a baby growing inside her wasn't bad enough in the first place, this baby had been conceived through rape and monstrosity. No good could come of that. She didn't have some loving husband standing by her to support her every move. She didn't even have her best friend anymore to guide her when times were as hard as they were now.

She was alone, soon to be caring for a newborn and a twelve year old girl.

She couldn't cope with this.

And yet she had to try, for Amália's sake as much as her own, and for the promise that she'd made to Viktória. That was another thing she would cherish dearly for as long as she lived. Stephánia had promised Viktória that she'd try to live. She had enough courage to honour the promise she'd made to her dead friend at least.

Amália's face soon appeared in her vision, the gaunt features reminding Stephánia of the mental torture she'd obviously endured. "It will be okay, Stephy." Amália assured her once more. "We'll go back to Ajka, we'll have our house back and we'll all live happily ever after."

Both Amália and Stephánia knew there was false hope in that statement. If they did return, Ajka would be gone. There wouldn't be the same small community where everyone knew everyone and there was no hostility running through the thoughts of every resident. It would either be a ghost town, or it would have been taken over by the anti-Semitic bastards who had sabotaged it in the first place.

There would be no Ajka for either of them, so there no point in entertaining the idea, yet they both still did.

Stephánia remembered how it had used to be, with her and Viktória carelessly gossiping every afternoon, because they had no responsibilities then; they had nothing to be scared of. She remembered Adrian and mused how she had always been so sure that Adrian and Viktória would be together forever, with tons of children all having a mixture of their features. Then she thought of Jakob and realised that Adrian could never have worked. So long as Jakob was somewhere, Viktória could never have been as happy with Adrian as she had seemed.

Amália remembered too. She reminisced on her time in Ajka with her twin. She and Renáta used to be the clowns of the village. With their undeniable likeness to one another they'd tricked everyone several times over - even their own parents. Having someone identical had its advantages and when either of them had done something wrong, it was always the other that got the blame. It was things like that Amália missed the most - not having Renáta to count on for anything. Her memories of Renáta were tainted now with the torture she'd endured under German instruction.

Amália also thought of Jakob. She hadn't known him, other than to remember that he was the one who had originally sent her to her sister's doom in the first place, with the help of the other balding man. From what Stephánia had said, Jakob had actually been a very admirable person and even she, who had had such bad experiences, could appreciate how much he cared for Viktória.

Amália had known Viktória as well and she had always liked the older girl. Viktória had been just as much of a big sister to her as Stephánia and Amália had been devastated to hear of Viktória's death as well. She couldn't imagine that Viktória could possibly fall in love with someone who was less than honourable. Especially not having loved Adrian like Amália knew she must have done.

Still, Amália couldn't find it in her heart to feel any kind of positive emotions towards the man named on Viktória's gravestone.

Stephánia stood up with a little help from Amália, still being weak and now burdened with the added weight of the child inside of her. Once again, she ran her fingers over the name, which was the only legacy of her life, engraved into the stone. She smiled to herself, but it was a sad smile, one that reflected how upset she was that Viktória was gone.

"We should get back for supper." Stephánia told Amália, finally turning her back on the stone and letting her eyes find the smoke that was rising into the air from the several fires that littered their refugee camp.

Amália nodded, also disregarding the headstone and facing in the direction they had come. "Yes," she agreed quietly. "You need to keep your strength up."

They traipsed back to the makeshift camp, Stephánia realising only now just how much more tired carrying a child around made her. When she'd first started making the trip from camp to grave, she'd been much weaker physically, but it had still taken less effort.

The added weight of her swollen belly was starting to really slow her down.

When they reached the camp the Soviets had set up for them, before moving on again to rescue more people who were apparently struggling in the same conditions, the smell of food instantly engulfed the two siblings. It was incredible to both of them how the smell of food still sent them over the edge like this, despite how long it had been since they'd been confined without barely a meal.

It did though, and they were at their own miniscule areas in no time, retrieving bowls of soup that were deliciously warm against their freezing hands. A friendly voice interrupted their silence a short time afterwards. "Back already?" He asked, a heavy German accent colouring his voice.

Stephánia turned around and smiled at Matthäus, the Jew she'd met shortly after settling into the Soviet camp. "Yes," she admitted. "We set off later than normal and we didn't want to miss dinner."

Matthäus smiled. "Of course." He agreed. "Do you mind if I join you?" He inquired politely, already knowing Stephánia's answer before she voiced it aloud.

Stephánia smiled immediately. "Not at all." She responded quickly, gesturing to the seat beside her. "Take a seat."

Stephánia regarded Matthäus once again, as she had everyday since he'd started eating his dinner with her and Amália, and was still startled by how good he looked. Considering the fact he was supposed to have stayed in the concentration camp with her, he had been surprisingly muscly from the first time she had laid eyes on him. When she'd mentioned it subtly, he told her he'd only just come when they were forced on the death marches.

Stephánia was pleased, because that meant Matthäus hadn't witnessed the same horrors she had and only endured a meagre portion of what would have been. She had found herself getting closer to Matthäus the longer they were together, but she didn't mind. Matthäus was nice and he'd been there for Stephánia all that he could. He'd even helped her with her pregnancy to a certain extent, and his words of wisdom inspired her everyday.

Matthäus sat sipping on the boiling soup he'd just fetched, watching Stephánia with the same guilt he always felt gnawing at him when he spent time with the girl. If she knew the truth about how he'd survived, about who he really was, then she'd hate him. But, he couldn't risk losing her friendship now. She'd come to mean a lot more to him than he'd ever expected.

When the death march had been announced amongst the officers at Auschwitz, Matthäus had known that it was the end of the camp. The Soviets would find them eventually if they were looking, so that was when he'd come up with his master plan.

He'd stolen some of the battered clothing the Jewish people had been forced into and modelled as one of them, shielding his face as often as he could and sticking around the men who wouldn't recognise him. He'd even gone as far as to tattoo a number into the side of his arm - he'd have easily been recognised otherwise. It had been considerably less neat than the majority of identification numbers, but he hadn't been pulled up on it, so he presumed everyone thought the tattooist must have been drunk.

He glanced at Stephánia again and held in a wince. He'd posed as a Jewish convict from then on, living on the meagre rations for only a day before the Soviets had caught up with them and he'd been rescued, no one ever suspecting that he had been one of the monsters helping to put them away in the first place.

He'd sought Stephánia out after that, having recognised her as Jakob, and mainly Viktória's, friend. He thought he owed them to look out for her, even if he probably wasn't the best candidate for it. Then, the bomb had been dropped that an abuser had planted a child in her. He'd felt even more responsible for her then and stuck close to her side through everything.

Matthäus had been to visit Jakob and Viktória's grave with her - though it had been incredibly hard not to show any recognition that a man he used to call bruder's headstone was in front of him. He'd kept any leering men away from her, protected her from all the japes and jeers that had been aimed her way after her pregnancy had begun to show.

And all the while, his feelings for Stephánia had steadily grown in intensity.

But she still had no idea who he really was, and she'd hate him forever if she did. Matthäus was doubly a traitor now and he didn't deserve her affections, not that she'd particularly shown anything other than friendly gestures. He returned his eyes to his soup and tried to stop berating himself over the decisions he'd made. If he hadn't, then he'd be dead and Stephánia would be in a much worse position - or so he liked to tell himself. By thinking that he'd helped her out that much, Matthäus managed to satiate at least some of his guilt.

Amália stood up once she'd finished her bowl of fresh soup and offered to take her other two friend's bowls back to be washed as well. Both accepted gratefully, especially Stephánia, who found that she was much wearier than she had any right to be.

Once Amália was gone, Stephánia shuffled along the hard ground closer to Matthäus and then rested her head tiredly on his shoulder. It took great restrain for Matthäus to stop his hand wrapping around her waist in a possibly unwanted gesture.

Stephánia let out a long yawn and Matthäus chuckled. "Tired?" He inquired teasingly.

"Like you wouldn't believe." Stephánia admitted, holding her hand up to her face as she yawned again, trying to make the gesture slightly more ladylike. Then, she let out a small squeak and both her hands flew instantly to her swollen stomach.

Matthäus glanced at her panicked face worriedly. "What's wrong?" He inquired anxiously, hoping that she wasn't having any kind of complications that might risk her health.

She glanced up at him, all the panic dissipated from her face and replaced with an excited quality, one Matthäus wasn't sure if he'd seen on her face before now. Instead of answering him vocally, Stephánia boldly grabbed Matthäus' hand and brought it to her stomach.

She smiled encouragingly at him and he moved his other to join it, just as the baby kicked against his hands. The feeling was weird, but somehow pleasant and he grinned at Stephánia - more pleased to see that she was genuinely happy than the fact he'd felt her baby's movements.

"It's amazing." She muttered, awed, as the child moved again. She was more surprised that she enjoyed the feeling than the acknowledgement it was actually kicking. She'd been so against the thing inside her that she'd never really considered the prospect that she might eventually come to love the baby. She associated it with the man who'd raped her countless times, she hadn't thought she could ever feel anything but hate towards it, but that definitely wasn't the emotion passing through her mind now.

Stephánia gazed up at Matthäus with tears in her eyes. "It's okay." Matthäus soothed her with such gentleness he didn't know he possessed, wiping away a few stray droplets with the pad of his thumb.

A smile touched on Stephánia's lips, and she leant into Matthäus' hand, which had gone to cup her cheek. "I'm going to love this baby." She decided. "I don't care who's it is, other than mine. I can care for it and I will." She decided resolutely.

"I'm glad." Matthäus agreed, not sure whether he really meant that statement or not. Obviously he didn't want to condemn a child that Stephánia hadn't wanted, but he wasn't quite ready to accept the fact the baby had been conceived so despicably yet. Part of him knew that was because he wanted it to be his own child. "You'll be a great mother." He knew that bit was the truth. From the way Stephánia acted around Amália, Matthäus couldn't doubt the fact Stephánia was good with children.

"I can't do it by myself, though." She suddenly averted her eyes and Matthäus knew where this was going. He felt his own breathing hitch as she said the words. "I don't think I can do it without you, Matthäus."

She raised her gaze again so that it pierced into his own and he knew that he couldn't deny her, even if he'd wanted to - which he didn't. "I'll always be here for you, Stephánia." He stated seriously, rubbing his thumb against her cheek softly, feeling the guilt nag at his conscience once again.

Stephánia smiled and in a moment of sudden boldness, she reached up and planted a swift but sure kiss on his lips.

"I wouldn't want you anywhere else."